Dig Pie Eye

By

Ade Annabel

This edition published in 2018 by Annabel Arts.
First published in 2017.

Copyright © Ade Annabel 2017

Cover artwork and chapter headings 1, 3, 6, 12 & 13 by the author.
All other chapter headings from Cornish paintings by Jacqueline Annabel which are Copyright © Jacqueline Annabel 2017.

A CIP catalogue record for this book is available from the British Library.

ISBN
978-0-9955922-0-9 (print)
978-0-9955922-1-6 (epub)

1. Battle of the Dinner Plate

Ursula Bull, a ruby lipped lady with a carefully coiffured side-sweep of ice blonde hair, seemed curiously ungrateful at having to retrieve the remains of a hot lobster from where it had dived for shelter in her ample cleavage.

'Everything was going fine until I made the mistake of standing up', Johnny Stern explained to the world in general and to Ursula's wide eyed dining companion, Bryan, in particular. He had unexpectedly been thwacked across the jaw by Johnny's flailing ankles and scuffed winkle pickers as he was trying to enjoy a quiet lunch in the Golden Lion nestling in Port Isaac's secluded harbour.

Johnny's lank grey-white streaky hair was temporarily lying in the spilt beer on the table, with his face twisted towards the condiments and the menus. His angular bony rear end was pointing straight into Ursula's red face. A pair of crimson triangular blushes on Bryan's forehead and jaw indicated where the twisted impact a pair of dirty heels had recently struck.

'The floor *is* very uneven', added a tall dark haired man who had been at Johnny's side and who now helped to peel him gently off the table. The bar staff began to gather nervously in anticipation of being requested to fetch another lobster, mop and bucket, or having to throw everybody out into the street for a general brawl. They hoped it would just be the mop and bucket, as the other two options would be expensive and disruptive to other customers.

In fact throwing out paying customers was never really an option for the Golden Lion, no matter how outrageously they behaved; especially if they were regulars and Johnny was as regular in Port Isaac's drinking establishments as night follows day.

Bryan stared down at his food spattered white tee-shirt and gold necklace and spluttered, 'Ot the 'ucking 'ell do you 'ink you're doing'. He seemed to have swallowed most of his consonants, not his food, and was clearly in no mood for Johnny's apologetic, 'Sorry old boy, didn't know it was your wife. Thought I'd tripped over a pile of coats left by the door. Is she wearing a fur coat or is she just naturally hairy? Gosh, she's got a nasty scar on her neck as well, hasn't she?' Johnny had an unerring tendency to dig himself in deeper if the opportunity arose.

Guy Adamson, who had lifted Johnny off the table, had already finished his crab pâté and quickly threw three £20 notes onto the Bulls' table, then arm wrestled Johnny out of the back bar and into the side passage that led down to the beach. 'Already £60 down and no commission yet', muttered Guy, under his breath, as he hoped the North Atlantic breeze and fresh ocean spray in the harbour might have a beneficial effect on Johnny's sense of balance and ability to negotiate stationary obstacles.

Back inside, Angela, who works the summer season, was tidying up the Bulls' table and running off at the mouth in obvious relief, 'You mustn't mind old Johnny. He's famous you know. He used to be in War movies. He's probably the last of the old black and white film stars, well, bit parts anyway. You know the sort of film – the ones with submarines and warships and landing carriers and 'eroism on the 'igh seas. I've not seen any of them myself but my Mum gave me all her old VHS stuff to throw out or keep when she had to *downsize*. My Eric reckons there's no point watching black and white movies if we've paid for a colour TV license. In any case he says you can't see any blood and nobody gets dismembered. But my Mum swears by Johnny Stern. She thinks he's lovely. Mind you he's not so clever when he's had his double brandies but you mustn't mind him. He means no harm.'

Mr and Mrs Bull were not very interested in heroism on the high seas but they were quite interested in dismemberment. That only sounded fair and just. They also resolved not to eat in, or holiday in, or even mention, this part of Cornwall again. At least that was the gist of the conversation as overheard, and later recounted, by Angela to the landlord and by the landlord to the police.

What in fact Bryan Bull said was that he would put Johnny up on the gibbet in his barn and slowly slice his flesh off. Ursula blanched and simply said that it would probably be a good idea if they didn't eat in public again whilst they were in Cornwall during this trip. She kept flicking her hair to cover the left side of her neck as it was now obvious why she wore high shoulder pads and tended to sweep her hair over in a grand side-parting; neither of which had been seen since in these parts since fashion was dictated by American soaps like Dallas and 'Die Nasty'.

Guy walked Johnny along the beach towards the massive concrete breakwaters. These were crude vertical walls set at just under 45 degree angles to the harbour like a partially opened doorway to shut out the worst of the Atlantic waves. From some angles at sea the door to the Port must appear shut but apart from not meeting in the middle they are staggered at intervals to the cliffs with one 'door' slightly further out into the bay than the other so that any vessel shallow enough to make it into the bay can do so except at the lowest tide.

Johnny's dishevelled white hair blew around his ears as the two men walked on a raised path that had been partially eroded along the right hand side of the harbour looking out to sea. The concrete they were walking on was set directly onto rock but still the sea would periodically pick up chunks of concrete and aggregate and toss them on to the beach as easy as a baby tossing aside a dummy. Fifty foot above them small houses and an old school perched nervously at jaunty angles as if suffering from vertigo from the shallow cliff. Johnny also staggered slightly against Guy who held him firmly but politely under the elbow. Many main streets in Cornwall seemed to be called Fore Street –whether it leads down to a foreshore or is miles inland – and this was no exception although 'main' may be a misleading description for a street too narrow and twisty to pass another vehicle without a good deal of swearing, waiting, backing up and being overtaken by pedestrians.

The fisherman of Port Isaac use the slippery seaweed covered path along the shore side to gain access to a series of small pools that retain water at low tide. Nestled in these are wicker pots crammed with crabs waiting patiently to be carted off to fish merchants, hotels and restaurants. Behind the pools and beyond the Breakwater are a series of cave-like openings that run right under the houses above. A couple of tourists had entered one of these and were blinking as they tried to adjust to the sudden change in light levels. Then one of them shrieked as cold running water dripped down onto their head and neck from the apex of the roof above. The cave at the back of the crab pool tailed off into an impossibly small and wet slimy stone passage. This one was too small for anyone to get through.

'I guess you're in your element here by the sea', commented Guy who prided himself on his careful research in advance of meeting his prospective clients.

'Can't stand the stuff. It's the wife. Marjorie always wanted to retire to somewhere by the sea and I couldn't face Brighton or Bournemouth. Couldn't afford Brighton or Bournemouth! First wife took all the loot, damn her. She went to America and shacked up with some Czech dancer or so I'm told. Huh, the bouncing Czech. I say. The bouncing Czech, do you get it?'

Guy assured him that yes he did get it, and privately hoped that he wouldn't actually be getting one of these from his client.

The wind began to pick up and scatter the shallow water into banana shaped ripples across the sand. The sand, in turn, would drain and settle into interlocked wavy ridged patterns. The raucous laughter of the gulls jeered at them from the safety of the rocks and a small wet sheepdog at the water's edge discovered that chasing its tail really was fun. Would the dog sink its teeth in if it caught its tail? Presumably it would give it a playful nip, then let out a fake theatrical yowl and then start chasing it in the opposite clockwise or anti-clockwise direction.

Some children were playing in the crab pool trying to scoop up the quick darting blennies that hid around the sides waiting for the tide to come back and liberate them. These small dark ugly fish had bullet-shaped heads but moved with an incredibly instant and elegant turn of speed if a small child had the temerity to try to catch them.

Other families looked nervously on from the hard-standing apron of the harbour known as the Platt to see if they needed to rush down and move their cars from the beach before the sea engulfed them. The streets of the harbour were so narrow that some cars chose to park on the beach. But they needed to obey the same rules as any other transitory form of life exploiting the rich pickings in no man's land between on the edge between sea and land. If the small animals and fish didn't flow in and out with the tide every few hours they would die and be picked over by ruthless scavengers. Saltwater is also an unforgiving environment for the modern combustion engine but at least it makes for an idle diversion for people sitting eating and drinking in the horseshoe shaped gallery of pubs, restaurants and holiday cottages around the harbour. You can almost read the minds of silent couples idly staring out at the cars parked on the beach remaining bravely static as the sea approaches. 'Will the owners of that Porsche or BMW remember in time? I do hope not. I do hope they went for a long walk on the coast path without looking at the tide tables.' But usually they come rushing out of a shop at the last moment just to tantalise the onlookers. Some do-gooder will have pointed out that a large wet thing is starting to get familiar and lick their axles. 'Spoilsports,' someone mutters as the car spins pebbles in a sudden rush back to safety.

'So it's a seaside garden you want?' asked Guy. He thought it was time to raise the reason he had travelled down to meet Johnny Johnny in the first place.

'Yes – we saw something on the telly the other day about the dearly departed Derek Jarman and his garden. Bit experimental of course, for my taste, but a cracking interpretation of Shakespeare's ambivalent sexuality, not to mention his weird take on religion. What a spanking shirtlifter!' Guy looked puzzled. 'Oh sorry…the garden, not the film called 'The

Garden'. Both superb. Makes Dungeness power station look like the Tate Modern. It was all driftwood, pebbles and natural English coastal plants. Stunning setting. I said to Marjorie that we should just get the deck chairs out and if we wait long enough the wind, the rain and the erosion and everyone around here will have one of those gardens.'

'I've not been to Jarman's garden but since he died I have seen it on the telly a number of times. I found it inspiring as it really brings the whole beach landscape into the garden rather than trying to keep it out and impose an artificial environment of herbaceous borders, lawn and roses. Of course it's at the opposite end of England and it's a very different terrain from here. It's flat open shingle for a start and not the beautiful rugged dramatic hills and volcanic rocky coastline you have. But, yes... I'm sure we can give you a Cornish flavoured version of a natural seaside beach in a garden setting. Can we see the site?' Guy asked.

'Yes – we have to walk though. There's no point trying to get a car up through the back streets here.'

The two of them started back up to the top of the beach and up through the narrow twisting pedestrian alleys that snaked between the odd shaped fishermen's cottages. Guy had brought a map and tried to trace their progress through Bloody Bones Yard, along Squeezybelly Alley (at just 18 inches wide Britain's narrowest thoroughfare), up Dolphin Alley, up Rose Hill and past the triangular house known as the Bird Cage. 'We're going to have some fun getting Bob's truck in here', he thought to himself.

'Here it is', said Johnny as he lurched up a side alley and into the back gate of a quaint, slate-roofed, whitewashed cottage. All the buildings in the old part of Port Isaac looked as though they had been built under the influence of alcohol. There appeared to be scant regard for the horizontal or vertical conventions of architect designed buildings that might have been planned and built all in one go on a flat, green field, site. The cottages ended up facing in every direction but were also often attached and huddled close together as if they were bracing themselves against a more than occasional salt-stinging gale – a bit like a colony of highly individual penguins pooling their collective body heat. The only difference with the cottages is that they couldn't take it in turns to be on the outside of the community facing the sea and wind – if they were built facing the North Atlantic they were stuck with it.

Port Isaac has some of the natural advantages of the mild South West of England, if you accepted that you were still in England when you cross the River Tamar which forms the boundary with Devon. The narrow separation of water, and the fact that you are never likely to be more than 10 miles or so from either the North or South coast, makes Cornwall seem an island rather than just an isolated peninsula. At least, that is, once you are into the proper part of Cornwall past the No Man's Land gateway of Launceston, the furthest into Cornwall that Justices and Offices of the Crown are traditionally said to have felt safe to venture and therefore the limit of English repression.

To British people on holiday, who habitually or occasionally don't want to venture to foreign climes in the height of summer, the far South West of England can seem almost sub-tropical. Even in the depth of winter the unwelcome attention of frost and snow tends to be rare. Throw in a dash of global warming and local gardeners can afford to be adventurous with your choice of plants. But on the coastal fringes they need to bear in mind the wind – the searing, salty, biting, unforgiving wind - that stunted the trees and bent them to a 45 degree angle. It also scorched and withered any plant with the temerity to grow lush green fleshy leaves into the teeth of an onshore wind. They ending up looking like brown paper bags ripped and blowing in the wind.

'The garden is around the side – through here'. Johnny led him down the narrow space between two buildings that opened out onto a broad, but shallow, lawned terrace with a death defying view over the harbour cliffs and roofs of the cottages below.

'We like to sit out here with our G & T's and Pimms. Would you like one? I'm getting a bit thirsty myself.'

'In a bit, perhaps. I just want to take some measurements and photographs.' Guy started about his business as Johnny continued to talk, totally oblivious to the fact that Guy was now completely absorbed in his own silent world of calculation and blank contemplation. The terrace was primarily a long oblong of close mown grass with a few plastic chairs at one end. Around all four sides, as if scared not to have their backs against the wall, were a few fading hydrangeas and fuchsias. Pretty enough, but to Guy it was no more than an empty, un-primed, canvas.

After what seemed an age, but was probably no more than five minutes or so, Guy began to surface from his reflections and tune back into the one sided conversation 'Can't mow the grass anymore. Have to get a chap in. Nice enough fellow but charges an absolute fortune just to lean on a machine and walk up and down. Outrageous. You'd think he'd be grateful for the work but I have to practically beg him to come around. Bloody gardeners. Oops, sorry. Nothing personal.'

With a slightly pragmatic and patient smile Guy concurred. 'Yes, I know, it doesn't take a lot of skill to set the cutting height of a mower to 1, 2 or 3,' although privately he suspected the high price the gardener asked for was to pay for his ear defenders to block out the mind-bleeding drivel he was likely to receive from Johnny. 'I should be able to give you some drawings and outline costs by the end of the month if that's okay?' asked Guy.

'Capital.' There was nothing more to say...for now. Guy had got his brief and was anxious to get back to his little studio tucked away in the Dorset hills where he could sit and dream and stare out of the window thinking about all the wonderful plants and designs he could create. But he also knew he would have to hire in some help for the actual installation, particularly if he wanted to turn this job around quickly and get in some much needed funds.

First on the team sheet when he was back in Dorset was Bob who was set to be the muscles in Guy's gardening venture and an altogether different character from the polite and diffident Guy. Key to maximising what he could spend on the garden would be getting good (by which Guy also meant cheap) labour. Bob Conan had a bit of the look of the rabbit, Dylan, from the Magic Roundabout but his manners were closer to those of Genghis Khan. He had a straw-coloured, platted, pony tail loosely connected to his bonce with a variety of rubber bands and agricultural twine and his main contribution to gardening was normally to offer to pee in your compost to improve the quality. Guy would refer to him as 'Conan the Barbarian', but if he was feeling particularly vexed or playful he might risk calling him 'Barbie' for short. Bob was definitely not the best person to put in front of the client until the cheque for the first payment had been cleared but he was a wiz with hard landscaping materials and could make the most incredible sculptures from the most unpromising junk. And he was strong. And he had a truck.

He had subcontracted the building of a conservatory to Bob a few months ago and discovered they had some mutual interests. Bob was trying to get out of being a jobbing builder and do some more creative work. When he met Guy he was toying with the idea of trying to sell wrought iron sculptures. He was also using a lot of found items from car junk yards and welding them into fantastic bird like shapes. They discovered they shared a delight in placing surreal and intriguing objects in a garden setting and as Bob's Japanese cranes made from parts of old Hondas were not exactly going like hot cakes they formed a cunning plan over a lunch strongly fuelled by their other mutual passion – real ale – to form a gardening business. Guy had never been confident with hard landscaping. First and last he was a plantsman. So it seemed a good idea to form a partnership with someone who could understand the beauty of different textures and materials; but not be shy of wielding a sledgehammer and driving a truck. It would certainly cut down his subcontracting costs which seemed to have taken an unhealthy slice of the few commissions he had had so far. Nonetheless he hadn't had chance to take Bob up on the offer until now and he wasn't at all sure if he would still be interested.

He rang.

No answer.

He waited.

He rang again.

No answer.

He rang a mobile number.

Disconnected.

'Why didn't he have an answerphone service?' Guy muttered. 'No wonder he doesn't get any business.'

Guy expected everyone, particularly if they aspired to run a small business, to operate in the same way as he used to in an office environment. It irritated him beyond measure that most people weren't just sitting by their phones and PCs waiting for him to contact them or have integrated voice and data message forwarding to mobile devices that were always on and available.

He rang again and then decided to jump in the car and go over to Bob's house. He tried to justify this to himself by saying he would do some shopping by which time Bob may be back home. He knew it didn't make a lot of sense but being fairly single minded and methodical he couldn't move on to the next task without finishing this one.

Piling into his faithful rusting green estate car, Guy set off down to Bridport along the coast road. It was a blazing sunny day and from the high vantage point he could see a ship, or possibly a tanker, miles out to sea on the hazy horizon. Guy's mind, though, was already designing a suitable driftwood sculpture for the garden in Port Isaac. He could see an overall shape but didn't know how to construct it or how it could be supported and anchored to the ground. He was still wanting to run his ideas past Bob as he pushed the supermarket trolley around ASDA. Consequently it was no surprise when he was in the checkout queue and realised that he had forgotten two of the items he really needed – an olive oil spread and some skimmed milk. Ah well, too late. Off to Bob's.

Bob lived in a typical builder's house. A front lawn littered with materials from half-finished and un-started projects. It was an ordinary 1950's pebble-dashed semi-detached on a Council or ex-Council estate. Most of it was now privately owned. Bob's neighbours had immaculate and attractive gardens. A little too tidy for Guy's taste but clearly much loved and deeply contemptuous of the eyesore over the other side of the privet hedge.

Guy knocked on the door. Then he spotted the doorbell and rang it. He was a little surprised, but not too surprised, when the doorbell chimed Wagner's 'Ride of the Valkyries'. He enjoyed it so much, although he loathed Wagner, that he rang it again and then again. It was tacky and tinny and he loved it.

'All right, all right, I'm coming, where's the flipping fire?' At least Guy thought he heard the word "flipping" as Bob emerged with white plaster lumps and powder in his wiry straw-coloured hair. The plaster was also smeared across his face and drifting like dandruff down from his shoulders. He used the back of his hand to brush some of his hair away from his brow but, stiffened by the dry plaster, some strands ended up in a stylish horizontal smear angled rakishly out from the side of his head.

'Oh sorry Barbie' said Guy, 'I thought you were out'.

Bob puzzled over this for a moment but couldn't let it pass. 'Yes I am' he said and shut the door. Just as Guy's finger was launched towards the doorbell for another valedictory blast of Wagnerian opera the door opened and it was grabbed by Bob's shovel-like hand. 'Got you that time. You're worse than the bloody kids down the street. Come in. I fancy a brew. And the name's Bob by the way.'

'So do I' Guy replied as he went in. He was ushered into the lounge and settled himself into a kind of giant leather poof that didn't seem to have any obvious shape or means of supporting the human body. As Guy wallowed in the undulations like a drowning sailor, Bob wandered back in with a couple of beers.

'I thought you meant tea', Guy stated.

'This is home brew. I know it's gone out of fashion a bit now. Too many bottles of wine that are really paint stripper disguised with a vague smell of parsnip but with these beer kits you can't really go wrong.'

'Oh, okay, I've made a will.'

A certain amount of sniffing, suspicious slurping, rolling of eyes and mutual 'Mmm's and 'uh, huh's followed before Guy finally pronounced, 'Hey, that's almost drinkable!'

'I should think so too – all the ingredients are fresh out of a packet and hand mixed by a trained expert, trained in reading instructions. Anyway what can I do you for?'

'Well…' Guy paused, 'you know we talked about going into the gardening business together…', pause for response, which was not really forthcoming, 'I've got a commission we could start on. It's down in Cornwall and I need your help. Are you up for it?'

Guy had meant to build up to this point slowly, feeling and cajoling his way to an irresistible proposition but when it came to the sticking point he felt that bluntness was best. All the same he was slightly surprised that Bob said nothing for what seemed an age although was probably only a few seconds.

'You'd better tell me about it first,' was the eventual reply.

'Well … it's in Port Isaac which is on the North Coast of Cornwall, half way between Rick Stein's Padstow and King

Arthur's Tintagel. But it's not as touristy as those places. It still retains the character of an old fishing village, just one with lots of tourists in it! I guess it's because it isn't really near a main road – it still feels remote. The commission is from a guy called Johnny Stern – a retired movie actor. He's a bit of a pain but no worse than any client. He's got a reasonably small but interesting terraced garden on a steep slope with great views overlooking the village and harbour. I had in mind a small sheltered area where he and his wife, Marjorie, could dine al fresco sandwiched between two grassy banks of wild cliff flora.'

'North Cornwall is slate country, right?' asked Bob.

'Yes.'

'So where are you going to use it?'

'I hadn't really thought about it yet.'

'And driftwood; have you got any?'

'I had thought about that but I don't know where I'm going to source the materials from yet.'

'I imagine they're probably a bit light on wooden shipwrecks these days. I guess it's more plastic that's thrown overboard but I bet you can still pick up a bit of natural or artificial driftwood and some pretty groovy rocks if you've a mind to. Probably quicker to make it myself with an industrial sander – the sort you get in boatyards. You could use slate to provide a flat picnic table and make sculpture piles with a few old lobster pots, buoys and pebbles scattered around the base.'

'Yes I suppose so.'

'Not much of a garden designer, are you? You have a commission but no idea what to put in it yet. I think you need some help … and not just psychiatric.'

'So you're up for it?' asked Guy.

'Of course I am. You knew I was. But not the psychiatric help. I really think you should see the professionals for that. And you know I'm not too hot with the planting. I know what I like but I can't speak Latin.'

'I've thought of that and I have an arrangement with Sparsholt College in Hampshire. They are sending a guy called Maya. In fact he should be arriving at the cottage this afternoon. Do you want to meet him?'

'Okay'.

The two new partners quaffed the dregs of their homebrew and set off back to Guy's house in his estate. Bob was silent on the journey although Guy passed a few pleasantries about the weather and local happenings but Bob was clearly thinking about ideas for materials. They pulled in to Guy's drive barely 15 minutes later.

'Cup of tea?' asked Guy as he locked the car.

'Yeah, why not?'

Guy rummaged through his selection of herbal and specialist teas before settling on a standard Tetley teabag in a mug. They walked out in to the back garden and surveyed the scene. Bob's eye roved around the surrounding hills.

Bob said, 'You've a nice setting here Guy, shame about the house.'

But Guy's focus was towards the bottom of the garden where he could see a small crouched figure by the dividing hedge. Guy walked forward. 'Er…excuse me!' he exclaimed.

No response.

'Excuse me!' Guy began to shout.

A small Chinese looking lady stood up from crouching. She had long black hair tied behind her head and in her left hand she seemed to be holding some seedlings.

'What do you think you are doing?' blustered Guy.

The small lady smiled, tilted her head to one side and then returned to a crouched position and proceeded to plant the remaining seedlings.

As Guy and Bob got closer she spoke, very softly, without turning her head. 'The English are so proud of their little homes like castles. You can't bear anyone to be on your property. I thought as I was waiting for you I would plant a few winter vegetables I had left over from seedlings and that I brought as a gift. They are Oriental. Very common but very good for you.'

'Ah…Maya. Stupid me. I was expecting a bloke. Don't know why. Pleased to meet you. My name is Guy. This is Barbie. He's going to be helping us with the garden.'

Maya stood up again, brushed some of the soil on her fingers onto her thighs and offered one still muddy hand. 'Pleased to meet you. Maya Mei'

'Pleased to meet you, the name's Bob,' he added as his huge horn rimmed fingers swallowed Maya's small palm. A slightly embarrassed silence followed and then Guy added, as if waking from a dream, 'Oh come in, have a cup of tea and I'll show you my plan for the garden in Cornwall'.

This time Guy proudly offered his full range of teas. Maya sighed, as if disappointed there wasn't more choice, and selected an English Earl Grey. The rough sketch plan that Guy had been working on was spread out on the kitchen table. Guy felt a little awkward about it now – seeing his plan through external eyes as he briefly described the Johnny's requirements. He apologised for the written notes, the crossing outs and the wobbly straight lines drawn freehand.

Maya was the first to respond. 'You say that the owners want to eat out in the summer.'

'Yes,' said Guy.

'Mmmm. You say they want privacy to left and right but an uninterrupted view of the sea and harbour.'

'Yes,' said Guy.

'But you also need shelter from the prevailing wind on the coast. Have you thought about a bamboo screen where it is already sheltered by buildings on the left, perhaps a Monterey pine feature on the right, where it is slightly more open rather than a Cypress hedge which will eventually obscure the view. As the pine matures it will keep on disrupting the wind at the top but you'll be able to see through the trunks at the bottom. And have you thought about planting some herbs and other fragrant plants by the seating area and some salad vegetables really close to the kitchen?'

'No,' said Guy.

'Mmmm. Just a thought,' Maya added.

Bob erupted with laughter. 'Glad to see we've got someone with some practical common sense. Guy tends to think about colours and **ambience.**' Bob rolled his mouth slowly around the word as if trying to swallow a New York bagel sideways. 'He forgets whether someone is going to want to walk from A to B in the rain and whether he's offered them the shortest route by putting in some hard surfaces and clearing the undergrowth. I want a slate table in the centre and I want to go beachcombing for some funky driftwood and bits and pieces to jazz it up.'

'Ah… remember Bob – you're the muscles not the brain. Don't get ideas above your station,' Guy quipped.

'I think I'll do just fine with Maya, thanks Guy. Your job,' Bob said, handing him an empty mug, 'is to keep the cups of tea coming and the client off our backs, eh Maya?'

Maya smiled and gave Guy her empty cup. 'What led you to take up gardening then Guy? You don't seem the type somehow? You didn't always work with your hands.'

'I don't know what you mean by "the gardening type". The one thing my career to date has taught me is that you need all types.'

Guy turned his palms up and looked at them. His hands were soft. His hands were clean. There was no dirt under his fingernails, no soil ingrained in his fingerprints and there were no calluses from constantly gripping the shaft of wooden and metal tools. He felt like an impostor. He replayed the initial handshake with Maya in his mind and recalled that her right hand was small and delicate but rough like sandpaper.

What was it that had led Guy here, to this point in his career? Now he thought about answering Maya's question he could see it wasn't a particularly logical move. 'I didn't mind the rat race', he said, 'it was just that I felt I had reached as far as I was likely to get and wanted to do something different.'

'Oh, the mid-life crisis!' interjected Bob.

'Perhaps.' But, thought Guy, it wasn't really like that. A crisis implied that something dramatic and exciting was happening. Guy was reasonably happy; he just felt that he was likely to fade gently into an anonymous grey oblivion if he didn't adopt a slightly different approach to life. That was all it was. For him it was an insubstantial whiff of ennui and a lack of motivation. It was an absence of interest in his career, rather than a blinding inspiration to do something wonderful and meaningful, that made him take up the trowel. He felt as if he was just a very small processing chip in a very large machine and was ready, indeed content, to be replaced by a new component built to an upgraded and improved specification.

What triggered the moment of change in the end was perhaps irrational, and trivial, and out of character for Guy, but to him it was hugely symbolic. He had watched a film called 'Groundhog Day' in which the main character, a TV weatherman, finds himself caught repeating the same day of his life again and again, no matter how he tries to change it – even by attempting to kill himself. What made it worse is that it was the third time Guy had tried to watch the film. On both previous occasions he had been interrupted about three quarters of the way through.

On the first occasion he had to get to bed in order to get up early to travel for a meeting the following day. On the second occasion he was interrupted by a long and involved phone call concerning a "Go Live" problem on some IT system. This time he was determined to see the whole thing through to the end so that he, like Bill Murray in the film, could finally break through to the next day and get on with the rest of his life. He watched the whole of the film and then, when he went into the office in the morning, he felt so elated that he resigned. The cycle was broken and he was free.

Frankly it had been a while since he could get excited about what was going on at work. He had seen it, done it, got the tee-shirt and it no longer felt like the real world to him. The real world was in the picturesque Cornish village of Port Isaac with a slightly cantankerous old man and a desire to make his little corner of the world look as good, in fact as stunning, as the spectacular coastal scenery deserved.

It was true there had been some heart-stopping and credit-stopping moments over the last year when an irregular income had caused him, and his loving dependants (like his ex-wife Julia, her solicitors Frank, Spurge and Docherty and his bank manager Mr. Epperstone) some deep-seated doubts. But he was beginning to get a reputation for quality and, perhaps more by luck than judgement, he was starting to get commissions like the one that had brought him to Cornwall. But the gap between success and failure was still agonisingly slim. Perhaps the formidable Julia would rather see him fail, than have the money – it felt as if she wanted both.

The day after Guy handed in his resignation Julia filed for divorce on the grounds of unreasonable behaviour. The divorce had been quick but incredibly acrimonious. Guy was even imprisoned for breaking into his own shed to 'steal' his gardening tools. Many of his previous certainties, including his naïve faith in the fundamental goodness of 'the system', had all but withered and died in those dark days. But strangely he was at peace and felt more certain than ever that he was doing the right thing. In his short spell in prison he became a great friend of the governor and used his influence to create a new and ambitious gardening programme for the inmates. It was regular work from the governor that gave Guy an income over that critical starting period, going back to the open prison to organise gardening working parties and bring them new seeds and plants. It also convinced him that it was something worth doing. He wasn't fooling himself that you could convert criminals into fine upstanding citizens with a little healthy exercise and the satisfaction of working with nature. But those people who already wanted to change were given an environment that would encourage them to be productive and those that didn't were at least given a break from the cells and a chance of some better quality veg.

Outside of the prison environment, with the few gardens that Guy had designed so far, he had tried very hard to make them unique to a particular time, place and circumstance. The individual plants or features may or may not be common but the fact that the particular combination of themes related to the local conditions, history, dimensions, aspect, people and historical style was something Guy took a great deal of care over. In his very first garden proper, for the governor's son, there were elements of the Victorian prison architecture and tales from some of the less savoury inmates that were used to influence and inspire the design. Sometimes these references were quite obscure and private, known only to the client, but he felt that every garden should be able to be read like a story... if the owner wished it to be told.

Guy felt that many garden designers tended to repeat a set of pre-packaged solutions that they had used before and knew would work, as if working to a formula based purely on size and cost. Eight metres by six metres square = diagonal wooden decking with ornamental grasses and metallic silver balls. Each of Guy's designs was rooted in the place and people involved, and seemed to grow organically from the geology and archaeology of the site but overlain with a scene or two from the customer's life story. So Johnny's allusion to Derek Jarman's garden hit exactly the right note with Guy. Undeniably Guy had a distinctive style, which tended to be loose and lushly planted, but it was not superimposed. His ambition, whether it was always achieved or not, was that the garden should fit the place and the people like a glove or more accurately many sets of different coloured gloves changing and shifting with the weather, season and evolution over time.

But there was still the awkward and practical business of converting an inquiry into a job of work. In the times that Guy had gone through this process so far it didn't seem to be getting any easier for him. He had to guess the budget that the owner had in mind. Then he had to double it (or at least see how much he could stretch it without breaking it). This would then be negotiated and scaled back to what he'd really had in mind in the first place. It wasn't the mechanical process of negotiation that he hated so much as the pressure to compromise on the quality of plants and materials, and to inhibit the freshness and style of his original design. But the thought of spending the summer working on the Cornish coast was just too tempting.

2. A Cunning Plan

So…committing pen to paper, Guy started his fine line drawing with a low protective arc of Golden Macrocarpus to shelter his exotics. But then, as if frightened to go further, he stopped and remembered his visit to the seaside village. He had a desire to know more about the birth, and growing up, of this place. Prior to his lunch with Johnny he had been browsing in the shops near the pub. He had come across some useful information amongst all the usual tourist blurb which purported to give information but were primarily adverts from places to stay, eat and play. Putting his drawing board to one side, he picked up a pile of these leaflets, plus a couple of more general books on Cornwall and settled down on the sofa to try and absorb some of the local culture in the hope that it might give him some ideas.

He read that the original Cornish language is similar to Welsh, Gaelic and French in reversing the English notion of word order. Consequently Port Isaac could just mean the Port belonging to Isaac or it could be a translation for the 'Port for corn' used by farmers rather than fishermen. It surprised Guy that the North Cornish coast would be able to produce enough corn for people to live on, never mind have a thriving export and import business, although he did see some evidence in the neighbouring Port Gaverne of where they must have dragged slate down to a crudely excavated dock and read about a narrow flat ledge behind the hill of Tintagel Castle that could have been used to import Roman and Middle Eastern goods from the very earliest times.

He looked up from where he was sitting, disturbed by the sudden alarm call of a blackbird in his quiet garden. 'Thank heavens there's no heavy industry here,' he thought aloud and then realised what a stupid thing it was to think. All around him must be robbed-out quarries. It was the stone cottages that first attracted him to this part of Dorset. 'I bet the tracks in this area must have thundered with the heavy carts taking their loads across country or down to the coast. In fact the best bits of London are probably built from the industry that must have existed here.'

He looked down and read on. The next port to Port Isaac, going south, was Port Quin, the white port, which had been virtually deserted since the majority of fishermen were drowned in a single terrible storm. Or so the story went. There had surely been many tragedies and drownings but Guy wondered if the decline in pilchard and herring was just as much to blame. Since the closing of the tin mines, fishing had remained the principle local employment, but increasingly, as at Port Isaac, this was becoming a faint tourist echo of its former self. Even some of the fish sold from the local fish cellars (not to mention the fish and chip shop) were stocked by van coming overland from other ports. Still Guy enjoyed seeing the small trawlers nodding on the choppy water in the harbour and watched whilst some crabs were being brought ashore like exotic parrots in their wicker birdcages.

Guy put down the leaflets, got up from the sofa and walked over to the large picture window to stare across the fields that could be glimpsed over his stone garden wall. He decided that he wanted to produce a garden that reflected both elements of the Cornish culture. One where the elderly and retired lived in a quaint old cream tea version of Cornwall alongside the more modern surfer's sandpit playground where 'Life is a Beach' and where Prince Harry, the young Etonians, and other public school toffs, get drunk on the Camel estuary at Rock and make themselves even more offensive than they normally are. Perhaps this was no more than an updated conflict between a quiet inward looking farming community living alongside an outgoing and adventurous international trade from travellers on the high seas amongst which there would always be a minority of pirates and wreckers.

Rather than settle on a single harmonious image of Cornwall, Guy decided he wanted to emphasise and highlight these opposing views of land and sea by developing a series of contrasts and conflicts in the garden. He picked up his fine line pen and started to sketch in some pebbles and a loose driftwood sculpture before marking the most sheltered area "Lawn". Garden designers always hate lawns in small gardens. They take a lot of maintenance and are distinctly old fashioned. Guy didn't care much for fashions. In any case, Marjorie had asked him for an area where they could spread out a blanket, and lie down out of the wind, to enjoy a picnic in dry weather. Guy had toyed with the idea of using a spongy base, similar to some children's playgrounds for placing under swings, but decided even a green one would look too much like tarmac. 'No,' he asked himself, 'what's wrong with a bit of grass with a traditional flower border?' He was obviously getting in the habit of talking to himself now he was living alone.

The artistry, he felt, was in the placing and shaping of the lawn and then being disciplined enough to choose a limited number of strong, contrasting colours and shapes to offset the flat sinuously curved green. He would use some traditional seeded annuals as well as the startling orange Day-Glo mesembryanthemums, some tall bronze and striped grasses, some white to palest shell pink hardy fuschias and some dark purple and cream violas. Behind it he sketched in some deep blue lacecap hydrangeas and a focal point formed by a cluster of five "Cornish" palms. The Cornish palms were in fact from New Zealand but they looked right and Guy had seen them for sale at the old Boat House as "Cornish". Further up on the South Coast across the Devon border they were also known as Torbay palms and they had been grown in this country for so long they have taken up dual nationality. Pleased with the resulting effect of this preliminary sketch Guy nonetheless decided to disguise and smudge the outline of the driftwood sculpture. He didn't want to be too specific at this stage as he knew Bob would probably want a hand in whatever the finished object looked like.

Guy always worked alone at this stage of a commission. Putting the installation into physical reality was a highly volatile and often noisy, frenetic and bad tempered collaboration with his colleagues and clients. But the thinking was done slowly, dreamily and often done alone. He wandered out from his back room studio to the kitchen, picked up an empty glass, and went out by the French Windows in the direction of a small brick Summer House which he had built at the end of a narrow but reasonably long garden. The door was already open. He slumped down on the wicker chair and felt underneath the loose cover for a box of bottles and a bottle opener. With the aid of a sparkling glass of local cider Guy squinted into the late afternoon sun and let his mind wander in, and around, the ideas for a new garden. He was soon joined by a troublesome tabby cat belonging to a neighbour but who seemed to have adopted the Summer House as his second home. This was the cat that had earlier caused the blackbird to panic and then adopted an innocent puzzled expression. 'Who, me?'

The Summer House was framed by a pair of old apple trees and looked out onto a small wildlife pond buzzing and droning with dragonflies. Occasionally a white Aylesbury duck would splash around in the pond and stir up the mud, but today Guy had safely penned her at the other end of the small Orchard near the yellow cob walls of the thatched cottage. Guy had only recently moved here and had had no chance to really develop his own garden. The estate agent had described it as an 'idyllic low maintenance garden in a beautiful setting' which basically meant that it was all laid to grass and would require a lot of hard work to make it into a garden that he would dare show to anyone. So far Guy had concentrated on building the brick Summer House, which was functional rather than pretty as it needed the clematis and passion flower to soften the bright bricks. He had made virtue of necessity by converting a deeply boggy patch of sunken lawn into a pond and put in a few reeds, iris and tall primroses. But the rest could wait. Commissions came first.

If only it were simply a question of getting commissions, thought Guy. He never charged for his drawings and the research required for his initial outline plans. Consequently he was currently finding himself doing a lot of work and not seeing much return. Some garden designers would never dream of putting pen to paper without payment but Guy figured that it was worth giving people a free sample. More often than not the client would then feel a moral obligation to buy. In any case he would never go into sufficient detail that a rival could pick up the design without having to contribute a lot of their own work.

More than this though, Guy felt it was his mission, his calling, to make people aware of the possibilities of their little plots and, of course, he enjoyed it. He believed that every place had a spirit, a genius loci, and that by finding out more of the tales of the people who had lived, loved, died, suffered, abused or murdered in a place you could set the changes and improvements into the context of the people and the natural history that had shaped that landscape. It wasn't just a question of slavishly following what had gone before – more often than not it was a conscious effort to enhance and modify it in a particular direction. People passing by when he was working on a garden would often say something like, 'How lucky you are to work with nature' and he would reply, 'I don't work with nature. I work against it.' But this was only partially true – he would work in sympathy with at least some of the plants that suited the soil and the climate and by studying the environment of the area select modern equivalents from similar environments around the world. Guy would get so angry when designers would just reproduce variations of the same award winning formula for any site and any person regardless of whether it was for a retired couple in Kent or a family of four in Manchester. They would just plonk it down as if it had arrived from Space and just shrink it to fit. He was still ruminating on the finer points of his design and on the iniquities of his competitors when he realised the sun had started to dip behind the roof of his cottage and he was hungry.

Eventually, after a week and a half, Guy's drawings were done. But he didn't feel the satisfaction of a job completed. It was now time for the moment of truth. He set off on the trip to Cornwall with some trepidation. True, he did have a complete set of drawings, elevations, prices and supporting explanations and project plans. He had a 3D virtual simulation of a garden walkthrough on his laptop and had rehearsed in his mind how he would present the ideas and the sequence of elements. But he was completely in the dark as to how the Sterns would react. He couldn't help feeling there was something wrong with this as a process. He should be able to check with them as he went along to see whether it was what they wanted before doing so much work. There seemed to be some sort of mutual mistrust between garden designers and their clients. The clients always felt that the designers would ignore their simple requests and tastes and produce their own overblown and pretentious project; which they already had had in mind to foist on whichever client came next. For their part, the garden designers felt that their designs would not be understood until built and maybe not even then. Guy felt that real garden designers weren't producing instant sets for TV makeover shows and Chelsea Flower Show because it would take several years for a good design to mature and be fully appreciated. The garden designer knew what was good for the client even if the client was too ignorant to appreciate it. Even as he thought it he knew it sounded arrogant and patronising.

Guy mused to himself about this love hate relationship as he drove down towards Devon. In many ways the gardener's approach to the client was worse than that of any Doctor Patient relationship. At least the Doctor would aspire to some kind of bedside manner even if the way they spoke to the patient was as an adult might speak to a child, not wanting to give them too much technical detail because they were too stupid to understand it. For the gardener their interpersonal skills were traditionally even worse – probably more akin to those of a surgeon. They operated on the garden not the client and their attendant anxieties. The Garden Doctor or Tree Surgeon would feel comfortable in a six foot ditch up to their armpits in tree roots and decking foundations; not discussing the secrets of their trade with the customer any more than a surgeon would want to show the patient how the first incision was made. During this second make or break meeting Guy had to get the all-important installation phase of the job underway, he had to get permission to operate. If necessary it would be under sufferance with a client that may be shocked, disappointed, suspicious or just seriously underwhelmed by the design.

As Guy passed Dartmoor and then towards Bodmin Moor the mists and the horizontal rain began to descend. Guy grimly squinted through the double speed windscreen wipers and pressed on. He just managed to catch the turning to North Cornwall and then the road which passed the invisible white giants of wind turbines outside the slate quarry crater of Delabole. Suddenly as he passed down the hill towards Port Gaverne the sea appeared at a turning in the road – bright and blue and clear. He could scarcely resist the temptation to drive over the field and straight down into it as he was so pleased to see daylight again. Finally he parked above Port Isaac with spectacular views along the coast towards Tintagel Head. Inland all was gloom and grey but out to sea it was a different part of the universe. The waves tickled rather than crashed against the cliffs whilst further out it was solid turquoise blue and calm.

Buoyed by optimism Guy knocked at the Sterns, having to juggle with his huge black portfolio and laptop bag on his shoulder in order to do so. There were a few spits of rain in the air as the house seemed to be right on the border between the two violently opposed weather systems.

The silver haired Marjorie opened the door, 'He's down the pub,' she said.

'Oh. When will he be back?'

'I don't know if he will be back.'

'Oh.'

'It's Guy Adamson. I telephoned.'

'Yes I know who you are.'

'Would you like to see the garden plans?'

'Yes but I agreed with Johnny that this would be his little project so I'd like him to see them first. I suggest you try the Golden Lion.'

'Okay. Hope to see you later.' Guy trudged off down the hill towards the Golden Lion. He wasn't particularly thrilled about the prospect of trying to spread his drawings out on beer, curry and fag ash stained surfaces getting lines where people leant on the side of the small tables and rings where glasses and ashtrays were used to hold it down. Perhaps he could persuade Johnny to come back to the house.

Guy looked in the public and lounge bars and couldn't see Johnny but hung around in case he was in the Gents.

'Perhaps the old bugger has been banned after all,' thought Guy, 'and hasn't had the guts to tell his wife.'

After a few minutes he decided to go down to the beach and watch the waves. This reminded him why he wanted this commission. There is something soothing for the human soul about simply being at the edge of land watching the reflections of the sky in still water or the gentle movement or sound of moving water whether it is the sea, a lake, a river, a pond or even a puddle. Perhaps we yearn to return to our amphibious genetic womb or maybe it is simply that sense of otherness created from being a land creature with a restless yearning curiosity. It may be a strong feeling that somehow we have been cheated of being able to effortlessly soar through the air or dive to the depths of the ocean and breathe underwater or maybe it is just a sense of calm tranquillity in the face of something that is unashamedly beautiful and serenely indifferent to our presence.

Reluctantly Guy turned away and re-entered the pub. Still no sign of Johnny. He asked at the bar. Normally if you ask a member of bar staff where a customer is you are likely to get a fairly blank look. Why would anyone expect them to remember all their customer's faces or names? But Guy guessed right. Both of the people behind the bar knew exactly who he was and, better still, where he was.

'He was in earlier. Had a few. Went off down to the Slipway,' the barmaid offered.

Guy had noticed the Slipway on his previous visit and knew where it was – the slipway was where the boats or vehicles made their way down to the beach and opposite the top of the ramp was the Slipway Hotel. It traded more as a restaurant and bar than a hotel and was next to the lifeboat house and opposite the fish cellars. Guy wandered off down there. Johnny was at one of the outdoor tables under a large canopy and heat lamp holding forth on some elaborate and convoluted story of his adventures to some unwitting tourists.

'There I was, tied onto the deck with only a flare gun to defend myself, as we headed into a gale, with the Scharnhorst coming up fast behind. I decided to jettison the fuel canisters from the port hold and hope I could get a clean shot in between the rolling of the waves. I dropped 6 fuel cans then came about hard. I was getting so close that I could see their captain on the bridge. He gave the order to open fire just as I levelled the flare gun at the nearest canister.'

'Hello Johnny' Guy interrupted, 'I don't think I saw that movie.'

There was a puzzled, then relieved, expression on the faces of the unwilling victims from Newport Pagnell as they realised that Johnny was just relating a movie plot rather than being attacked by Somali pirates or somesuch. Nonetheless, undeterred, Johnny sailed on to tell of his heroic but ultimately doomed battle to save his ship, his comrades and the so called lucky mascot who was a goat called Clive. Johnny's stories always seemed to reach a crucial point just as the bottom of his glass emerged from the hidden murky depths. He demanded a refill as payment on account for finishing his story oblivious to the fact that no-one had requested it. He was performing and expected to get paid.

Guy had to wait patiently until Johnny had completely finished and the couple who must have been in their early twenties made their excuses in order to go and find a sink to clean the vomit stains from their wailing infant. They disappeared off to the toilets in a whirl of wet wipes never to reappear. Perhaps they found a back entrance or, more likely, a big enough window!

Finally Guy had his man and, just as Johnny paused to take onboard sufficient fuel to start the next monologue, Guy took this opportunity to raise the subject of the garden plan.

'What? Back at the house with Marjorie? Are you mad? I want to get some audience reaction to whatever you're planning, young man. Come with me to the Golden Lion and show Jim, Tony and the lads.'

Guy, feeling that it was more than likely to be just an excuse for Johnny to finish his current drink, which was barely started, and order another one at the Golden Lion, had to demur.

'We really need to be in the garden or, ideally, looking out on it from the house. Besides I need to show you something on the computer and the battery is nearly flat. I need to use the mains.' he lied.

'Poppycock! You just want Marjorie there to call the ambulance and attempt the kiss of life after you've told me the price.'

'Well, that too.'

'Too mean to buy me a round.'

'If you order the garden I'll throw in a case, no a couple of cases, of Grade A plonk of your own choosing for the Grand Opening.'

'Now you're talking, young man. I think we're going to get along famously.'

Johnny manfully downed his drink in one (with some of it even going in his mouth) and the two set off leaning against each other like an A frame. This was hard for Guy because he had an A2 portfolio and an old heavy laptop to cope with as well as the swaying Johnny and a 1 in 5 slope back up to the house.

Falling in the door, Johnny made for the toilet whilst Guy, flexing his shoulder to encourage the blood flow to return, looked for a suitable table. The kitchen would be fine. It was spacious and airy with a stunning view of the hills on the other side of the harbour. Marjorie appeared in the doorway.

'I see, or rather I hear by the gushing fountain in the downstairs toilet, that you have managed to snatch my husband from the clutches of the demon drink.'

'Yes … and from his adoring public.'

'There you have it. I don't think it's the drink that primarily attracts him. It's the bright lights and the people. The roar of the greasepaint and the smell of the crowd or was it the other way around? You know he keeps telling people he was in the old black and white war films don't you? I know he's ancient but he's not quite old enough for that. I think the only black and white film he was in was a training film for the Armed Services when he was doing National Service. They had some old stock they wanted to use up.'

Johnny entered the kitchen.

'Well, come on man. Let's see the drawing.'

Guy began his preamble – reiterating the design criteria he had applied to the brief, to his understanding of the client's aspirations and why he had discounted a few of the options. Finally he started to unfurl the largest of the drawings he had brought with him (the bird's eye view plan) and laid this out on the table. This was always the most critical moment, although he had a few other tricks deliberately left in the locker. The design was deceptively simple from a vertical perspective. There were three main areas – all irregular lightly curved rhomboid shapes forced by the topography of the sloping site. Overlapping the site and between the three areas a series of larger and smaller abstract plant shapes sub-divided these three areas. They couldn't be described as garden rooms because it was impossible to screen the bottom from the top of such a sloping site.

As far as the Sterns were concerned what they were looking at was just an abstract pattern. It could have been a design for new wallpaper or a new tablecloth.

Guy outlined what the functions for each area were, how they were interwoven with planting themes and how the garden related to the buildings and the Cornish landscape beyond. The Sterns nodded, as if humouring him, but Guy was clearly not getting the kind of response that he was expecting. Even the normally vocal Johnny was taciturn and uncommunicative. Aware that the skin around his neck was becoming flushed and blotchy, Guy rushed to fill the silent void with an increasingly rushed torrent of irrelevant detail – plants he had rejected and later choices to be made of types of stone that the Sterns couldn't possibly visualise without pictures or samples.

Guy then covered the first drawing (ironically just as Marjorie had leant over to study it more closely and needed to quickly straighten her back and retreat a couple of steps). Guy showed the first of a series of elevations revealing how the garden would look in three dimensions. The view was from the large patio doors in the lounge from about settee height and must be one of the Sterns' most familiar views. Although it was based around a computer design with standard components Guy had loosely sketched into the background were the roofs of surrounding cottages with the harbour hill and glimpses of the sea beyond. The glass doorway was framed by a formal pair of heavy Greek amphora bolted at the base to a metal plate. Tumbling from these were a pair of hardy salmon-pink fuchsias. To the sides of the view through the glass doors were the tall elegant arching arrow-like leaves of the bamboo and further down on the right hand side were the twisted arms of specially trained Pines looking like overgrown Bonsai.

'It looks a bit Oriental,' pipes up Johnny.

'Yes – but this is only one view. There are bits of classical English, wild Cornish and a bit more Oriental in the planting of the salad area.'

'You know the Japanese are the enemy, don't you?' piped up Johnny.

Despite his usually almost limitless reserves of tact and patience Guy was finally starting to get a little flustered and annoyed that this wasn't going as he had planned it. When he rehearsed his presentation in the car, this was the bit where Johnny and Marjorie swooned with gasps of amazement at his stunning fusion of Oriental and Classical influences to form an imaginative, modern multicultural harmony.

He responded in a slightly exasperated and superior tone as if scolding a naughty child. 'The Japanese aren't the only nation to have picked up some of these influences. In terms of historical style the Japanese took Chinese ideas the same as the Romans adopted and adapted Greek ones. They merged it with their own ideas and exported it successfully to other nations who in turn adapted and changed it again. I've been taking a bit of a lecture on this lately from a lady called Maya who I hope you will have the chance to meet.'

'I'm not having some slanty-eyed bint in my garden!'

'Johnny! Don't be ridiculous!' cried Marjorie, 'At least give Mr. Adamson the courtesy to finish his presentation before making any judgements.'

'I will insist on Maya coming if you want me to do this garden. Shall I go on?'

'Yes Guy – please do,' Marjorie insisted.

'Hrmph,' added Johnny.

'Here's another perspective: one from the alleyway running along the bottom of the garden. You will get a lot more privacy in the lower area and the ability to dine out or laze out in the sun without being overlooked. This is the perspective diagonally across the garden, showing the impression of greater size given by breaking the space into three main areas, with focal points in each stopping your eye from seeing everything at once. Let me show you the 3D model simulated on the laptop.'

Guy outlined some of the features and then allowed Marjorie to move the mouse around the virtual garden herself. He clearly had one convert and he could feel, but not see, the blood near the surface of the skin in his neck beginning to reduce in colouration. 'This is really easy. I have been going on to Johnny about getting a computer but he thinks they are the work of the devil. Probably Japanese devils at that.'

'Yes it is. If you like I can leave the laptop with you for a while to look at the designs. Everything that's on it is synchronised with my desktop computer at home and it would be useful to have a soft copy of the design with the software here in case we need it to make any changes on the fly without pulling big files over your broadband network.'

'Oh would you leave it here? That would be great. But we haven't got any broadband. Johnny again. Have you got Word and some games?'

'No games I'm afraid, but all the standard Microsoft stuff – yes. You'll need a printer of course if you want to write any letters but I could bring a small LaserJet with me when I come back if you like and I'll bring a dongle or something so you can try the internet on my account. It would be useful for me, to be honest, so that I can make a note of any changes to the design and keep in touch with my email.'

'Sounds like you've got the job then Mr. Adamson,' said Johnny, 'and I haven't even asked you the price yet.'

'Well it depends a little on the final choice of materials but here are some indicative budgetary costs. Unlike builders I like to sign a fixed price contract when we've agreed the specification. The materials can be given a price tolerance or pick from a catalogue menu if you change your mind on individual items but I won't charge you any more labour no matter how long it takes. I think it is important that people can see an end in sight and not feel that they are signing an open cheque. Nonetheless I would like to ask you for a 25% deposit to secure Bob and Maya to work for me. I won't be taking anything myself until the job is completed to your satisfaction.'

'There's something missing though,' said Johnny, 'I want to feel at home in this garden. I have a few props from some of the sea battles I have been in which I keep in the shed. Some wheels, pennants and a machine gun emplacement.'

'Okay. I'd like Bob to take a look at them. He's a bit of a wizard at making sculptures out of found objects. Yes, I'm sure we can come up with something on the theme and there's definitely room where I was thinking of putting some sort of statue or sculpture in front of the Pines.'

'I think this calls for a Pink Gin. When can you start Guy?' asked Marjorie.

'I can start drinking right now,' said Guy with a twinkle in his eye.

Guy agreed to start in a couple of weeks and left the house feeling elated. Before leaving entirely, he decided to take another look around the outside, particularly at the boundaries. He was a bit concerned about the logistics of getting heavy materials on to site and whether he put enough contingency into the quotation to cover crane hire if he needed it.

Guy wandered up the left hand side of the house. Johnny appeared at the side door to put a few empty bottles into a box ready to take to the Bottle Bank up in the village car park. Johnny spotted Guy and lobbed one of the bottles at his head. Or at least Guy thought he had. The bottle smashed against the house opposite with a resounding and satisfying tinkle.

Out of the other house emerged a florid-faced, wild grey-haired, man incandescent with rage. 'Stern! I swear one of these days I'm going to murder you.' The door slammed shut again behind him. Only then did Johnny notice Guy. 'Thought you'd gone. What are you up to?'

'Er... I was just checking how to get materials into the garden. Actually I was hoping to bring them in across your neighbour's, as his house has access to the wider of the two lanes. I thought it would be better to park the lorry for deliveries on that side as there should still be enough room for an ordinary sized car to squeeze through.'

'Ha. He'd be only too happy to oblige. As long as you tie him up on a bamboo cross and torture him within an inch of his life.' Johnny then slammed his door and presumably returned to his gin cabinet.

With a sinking feeling Guy sloped back off to the car park and set out for Dorset. 'What have I agreed to?' he thought, 'Is it too late to pull out? Do I really want to work for a mad drunk with a film fixation?'

Then, as he was looking in his rear view mirror at the blue Atlantic receding behind him, he thought, 'ah well, takes one to know one I suppose. Plus my bank manager says he's a bit short this month so I guess it would only be fair to give him something to tide him over.'

3. Saints, Shrines and Sinners

Two weeks to the day Bob, Maya and Guy set off for Cornwall. The plans had all been agreed, the materials chosen, the suppliers notified and the materials ordered.

The three were in good spirits, sitting and swaying side by side in the cab of Bob's lorry and singing 'We're all going on a Summer Holiday'. Bob and Guy were anyway. Maya didn't know the words, or why the other two were insisting she was the spitting image of someone called 'Una', but was nonetheless caught up by their infectious good humour and her own sense of embarking upon a new adventure.

It was actually a bright Spring day, full of chilly promise, with crystal-clear views of the surrounding hills and fields. Fortified by an overdue Cornish Pasty and Chips from the Cornish Arms in Pendoggett, the three eventually rounded the corner above Port Gaverne to an absolutely stunning blue meridian expanse of sea, framed underneath by viridian green hills dropping out of sight over cliffs to the ocean, and topped by a clear blue skies with narrow wisps of creamy cloud.

'I think a fellow could get used to this place,' intoned Bob.

'You wait until you see how close you can park to the site,' said Guy.

They struggled and backed up and re-manoeuvred, and squeezed, and asked people to move cars, until they got to the lane outside Johnny's neighbour's house. Guy took a deep breath, swallowed, and marched up to the door. The other two sat in the cab and waited. They could see Guy from the back talking to a highly animated figure on the doorstep. This person gestured and shook his fist in the direction of the Sterns. After a while Guy came back to the cab, put his head in the door and said, 'Right then. All set. You can start bringing stuff in through the neighbour's garden.'

Maya and Bob looked puzzlingly at each other, then back to Guy, back at each other, shrugged and then got on with it. Whatever difficulty or deal or compromise Guy had come to with the neighbour it seemed he wasn't about to tell the others. Bob had a theory though. He decided to keep an eye on this 'neighbourly' neighbour.

The three of them worked on until Sunset. The Sterns had booked a holiday and wouldn't be back for a couple of weeks. This suited Guy and Bob. There was an outside tap. They had a camping gas stove to brew up the endless mugs of tea and local public conveniences to deal with the inevitable overflow. They were as happy as pigs in dirt ripping up the previous garden, measuring, digging, levelling everything and laying out the stark skeleton of the hard landscape design.

Maya was at a bit of a loss though. She found the male 'buddy buddy' camaraderie and banter of the other two a bit exclusive and a bit too 'blokey'. She also didn't have a lot to do at this stage. Although she was used to hard manual labour, and could more than pull her weight, a lot of the work at this stage was still logistics and contemplative refinement of the planning. The other two would seem to rest on their shovels, or sit drinking tea discussing the job for ages, whilst Maya would get more and more frustrated. She looked forward to getting on to selecting, and laying out, the plants. That was her favourite activity – particularly the choosing. She would go to a wholesale nursery and study row after row of seemingly identical plants and be able to pick out just the right ones that were perfect for the site. They wouldn't necessarily be the largest or the brightest. She could pick the hardiest, or the one with the best shape, or the one with the most bud rather than the most flower so that it had real impact but more slowly over a longer period of time. Plus she would also always want to come back with a bonus. Something that was out of season but that would complement the design and that she hadn't thought of before. Perhaps some bulbs that would be invisible for a few months and so not affect the structure but provide the perfect colour complement at the right time.

She was standing around on the morning of the second day, looking out from the small garden towards the sea, when Guy looked up from digging and seemed to notice her for the first time. He put his shovel down and padded softly over towards her. She noticed him and half turned. He smiled and took her small palms between his soiled and grubby thumb and forefingers, tentatively suggesting she might like to take the opportunity to explore the village and some of the tourist shops and attractions whilst the groundwork was being completed. Maya's heart soared at the opportunity and readily accepted, but not to go trinket hunting.

Maya wanted to find out more about what made Cornwall different from England. She had never been this far west before, having spent the last few years in East Anglia. When people asked her where she was from she would sometimes respond that she was from the mystic East by which she meant East Anglia. In truth she had only arrived there from Hong Kong as a young teenager, and her knowledge of Britain was largely from novels and TV, before she had left home in Norfolk fairly recently for central southern England. She had started to read a copy of Daphne du Maurier's Jamaica Inn that she had picked up at the library before coming on this job. This made her want to hear tales of fishermen, of smugglers, of excise men and strange goings on by flaming torchlight on Bodmin Moor. She wanted to speak to Cornish people to see if she could find anyone who still spoke the language. She wanted to find out about local customs and about the people's history.

Instead of heading into the bay, and looking around the seaside, she headed off to the church near to where she was working on the premise that it was likely to be the oldest building with the greatest connection to Port Isaac's communal history. She went in and was slightly disappointed. Even to her untutored eye it did not look as old as she thought it should. It wasn't modern. But it also was not what she was expecting. She had imagined some sort of portal through which she could step straight back in time into medieval England. Certainly the churches near the Agricultural College where she studied were like that, and so were the ones where her family lived. She looked around at any features and ornamentation she could find for some clues. None of the dates reached far back in time.

A round mole-like lady in a dark brown coat had come in and stood with her back to the aisle. As Maya watched her she turned around to reveal a pleasant face and huge round plastic glasses. She enquired if she could be of assistance to Maya in a loud, simple, shouting version of English. Perhaps she assumed Maya was a foreign tourist. If in doubt of being understood the English tend to just raise their volume as if megaphone baby-speak were a form of universal Esperanto. Maya asked if this was the only church in the village or whether there was perhaps an older one down towards the harbour. She was told that there were a few local chapels, some converted but the lady did not know how old they were. The lady speculated as to whether they were later than the church but added that Cornwall, like Wales, carries a strong tradition of non-conformist Christianity and so they could well be earlier or the same date as the Church of England.

Maya found this particular Church of England a bit stifling as if she felt she were a brightly coloured exotic bird caught and stuffed in a glass dome in a Victorian front parlour. She found and explored the Chapel across the other side of the harbour which was now a pottery and café. There were some beautiful vases with fluid, swimming, oily-looking landscapes painted onto porcelain and decorated in a gilded art nouveau style, but no clues as to what life was like for a remote fishing community before the invasion of the 4x4 Chelsea Tractors, television and the internet. There were two lanes where she was and she considered walking up them to explore. One followed the line of the coast and was called Roscarrock Hill and this seemed to ring a bell in Maya's mind concerning something the lady in the church had said about more chapels. The other went virtually opposite back in land and was called Church Hill. Bit of a clue there perhaps, she thought, so this is the way she went.

It was a long steep climb and Maya really began to feel an unfamiliar pull on her calves and thighs as she slowed and looked back around at the harbour below. The sensation served as a reminder to her of the time she had been loaned a bike by her college friends to go out on a picnic. Although she was pretty fit she hadn't ridden a bike since childhood and found that keeping up with the others revealed muscles she had forgotten she had, and they certainly felt as if they hadn't been used in the intervening decade. Nonetheless she kept up a brisk pace, anxious to see what was around the next corner and, every time she looked back down the hill, enjoying the site of the sea and the now distant toy houses from the port. The houses seemed to Maya to have grown up higgledy-piggledy, directly out of the earthy, hilly slopes. Their roofs were all jumbled together at odd angles giving her the impression they had fallen into place at the bottom of the hill during a landslip or an earthquake. The lapping of the waves at high tide were now too faint to detect but still the wind and the plaintive cries of the seagulls reminded her she was still at the seaside. She walked on, and on, and on a bit further on a winding hedge-bound road. It finally led through pleasant green pasture as the gradient began to settle a little more around the horizontal. But still no sign of a church!

Looking over the hedge into the field she saw a young farmer, quite close, extracting some old barbed wire that had become caught in the axle of his tractor. He was tall with short, wavy, blond hair. He had a blue checked shirt on which was unbuttoned to half way down his tight, muscular chest and wore surprisingly clean, almost starched, blue jeans. Maya asked him if he could direct her to the church. The farmer looked at her a little as though she had just beamed down from another planet but quickly adjusted and with a broad, kindly smile ambled over to the gate to talk to her.

'Are you down here on holiday?'

'No I'm working in Port Isaac.'

'Oh so it's not the church *there* that you're looking for.'

'No I've just come from there.'

'You're probably looking for St. Endellion then, you can see the top of the tower over that field, but I'm afraid it's a bit of a walk. If you want I can give you a lift when I've cleaned the tractor up and attached the trailer. My daughter, Ursell, is just making a mug of tea if you'd like one while you wait. You look as though you could do with it.'

'You noticed. Yes, I'm not used to these hills. It's very flat where I come from.'

'Where's that then?'

'Well, Hampshire at the moment and Dorset the other day but my family live in Norfolk.'

The farmer shouted into the open door of the farmhouse to order the tea and the collie tied up nearby began to bark wildly at the sound of his master's voice. Eventually the farmer went inside and came out after a couple of minutes with two mugs of sweet hot tea. He attached the trailer while Maya drunk her tea. She was very pleased to have someone to talk to and the farmer made a knowledgeable companion as they started up in gear with a jolt and then, with an enormous roar, splashed out of the farmyard puddles into the lane. Maya had asked him whether he enjoyed farming. He told her about the seasons (good and bad), about the wildlife, about the EU subsidies, about the Farmer's Union and about social life amongst the young farmers thereabouts.

Maya was interested equally in everything and asked all sorts of questions. Apart from quickly finding out that the farmer was called Diggory Brae, she was particularly interested in the different crops and whether they coped with the salt and wind. She also asked about life in times gone by, about local pagan customs in the early days of Christianity, but Diggory either didn't know or didn't answer these questions with much more than 'I don't know about that'. In any case they were now at the church. Maya thanked him and promised to drop by again on her way back into Port Isaac. He offered to give her a lift back down into the Port as he would be heading down to the Golden Lion. 'No, not in the tractor, you'd be travelling first class. '

When she arrived at the church Maya wandered around the graveyard trying to read what she could of the family names and inscriptions. It struck her as odd that many people found cemeteries uncomfortable, dull or desolate places. To her parents it had always been totally natural to treat her dead relatives with the same honour as the living. There was loss, certainly, and for anyone bereaved of close family or friends that loss could be unbearably raw and painful. But it was surely also a place to celebrate people. She remembered a great uncle who had died on duty as a firefighter. She had never met him but she remembered being taken to his grave by her parents and how absurdly proud they were that he had been buried in a part of Wo Hop Shek Public Cemetery called 'Gallant Garden'.

She wandered slowly through the graveyard at St. Endellion trying to read the fading moss covered inscriptions and reflecting that whilst the people here were dead, she, for a while, was not. In fact she felt more gloriously and fully alive, being able to visit the dead and then, unlike them, having the choice to walk away. She instinctively felt that there was no such thing as an ordinary life commemorated here. She fancied that the people here may have experienced the shock of seeing the first motor car, with someone walking in front waving a red flag. They may have had terrible adventures in the mines and been trapped underground for hours or days, only to emerge safely into the arms of loved ones. They may have simply lived out a quiet and unassuming life of poverty and struggle to feed their family, but whatever it was, she doubted that it had been dull or eventless.

Satisfied that she had seen all the graves, one by one, and having mentally made a note of a few recurring family names, Maya then entered the church itself. At first she had to adjust her eyes to the contrasting dark and light within the church and then she began to feel the calm peace and sanctity of an old church. Maya was not Christian but she was fascinated by the historical and cultural trappings of Christianity; she enjoyed the classic solemnity of the Saxons and Normans, the invigorating swoop of a young choir in full and unearthly flight or the rich gold leaf and lapis lazuli of a medieval manuscript. She felt the same in some modern churches but rarely in churches that had been built (as opposed to restored) in the Victorian era. She felt that most of these had all the breathtaking beauty and gravity of a municipal toilet block. Doubtless there were some stunning ones but Maya hadn't been to them yet and didn't particularly want to find them. She was happy right here, right now in this medieval space.

The pew ends were all elaborately carved in rich dark wood like plain chocolate. An impressive and grand cacophony of organ pipes was clustered at the far end and the whole tranquil scene multi-coloured by rich stained glass from which the light slashed diagonally across the nave. There was no smell of incense but nonetheless Maya found the atmosphere intoxicating and lost herself in the details.

After a while she had seen all she wanted and stepped back out into the fresh warm air. There were many questions buzzing through her head and they all seemed to centre on the mysterious saint mentioned in the church. St. Endelienta was her name but there wasn't much in the way of information about who she was meant to be and what she had done to deserve becoming a saint. Maya was surprised that Endelienta was a woman. Why wasn't the church called St. Endelienta? Even the name seemed to have become mysterious and lost in the fog of time. It was now Endellion; a much more masculine-sounding name. What she had read about Endelienta implied that she was a sister of a family of saints in this part of Cornwall and that there was some connection with Wales. It seemed that whatever culture this person belonged to it was definitely not English. It was Celtic and stretched from Scotland, through Ireland, Wales, Cornwall, on to Brittany and maybe even skirted the north and west of the Iberian Peninsula. This would make sense of some of the strange place names she had come across in Cornwall. The fact that Pen was used as a prefix as commonly as Pant or Pant Y in Wales – a name that had caused her teenage girlfriends endless amusement in all its variations on a coach tour she had once been on. Maya was so impressed that she had found a female saint that she resolved to find out more about this Endelienta.

She was beginning to feel a little hungry and so set out back to Port Isaac. She called in, as promised, at the farm but couldn't find anyone around. She knocked on the kitchen door and looked around where she hoped to find the daughter. There was no sign. In fact the only signs of life were the two mugs from earlier on the drainer and a plate from lunch. Maya called through the doorway, 'Hello, is there anyone around? Diggory?'

No reply. All she could hear was a piece of polythene caught under a gate in the yard which was tapping gently in the breeze and the distant sound of a skylark singing. There was clearly no-one around and so Maya went to look in the barns and outhouses. There were two of them. One large aluminium roofed structure with a concrete floor which looked like it might be a milking shed or containment area for cows – judging by the liberal spread of muck. The other, slightly smaller, seemed to be for storage of all kinds of equipment, containers and sacks of feed. She didn't like to go in and investigate too closely but there seemed to be nothing there. In any case she called out again, but there was no reply.

She made her way back across the muddy cow-trodden yard, slipping, and sliding, and cursing the fact that she had left her wellies in Bob's lorry. She had to steady herself a couple of times and wasn't looking up at all, just at the few feet of ground in front of her. Eventually she was approaching the outer gate by the road, and about to walk back down to Port Isaac, when she thought she heard a gentle, faint whimpering sound.

She turned her head to point one ear in the direction she thought she had heard something.

There was definitely something, but it seemed to fade in and out a bit as the wind changed direction. It sounded human. Not like a lamb or a cat. A kind of low moaning, but intermittent and dull. Her first thought was that maybe Diggory, or his daughter, had hurt themselves. Perhaps they had become caught or injured with one of the many fierce looking cutting blades on the trailers she had seen stored for ploughing and threshing.

Suddenly Diggory grabbed her from behind. 'What do you think you're doing?' he thundered.

'I…er…you asked me to call back. You said you'd give me a lift.'

'Why didn't you ring at the doorbell rather than come poking around?'

'Sorry'.

She wanted to say that she had heard something and to ask him if he had heard it. She also wanted to say that she had knocked on the door hadn't seen the bell. In any case she hardly expected to find a farmer in the house during daylight hours.

But she didn't say it. The red-faced, wild- eyed, Diggory in front of her now was not the same person she had talked to earlier and Maya began to feel unwelcome.

'Farms are dangerous places. You shouldn't go poking around where it don't concern you. Get in the Land Rover.'

'It's okay, I can walk.'

'No. You get in there. Dog won't bite. Unless you're wearing anything woollen that is. He likes to give the odd sheep a bit of a nip if they misbehave.'

Maya was reluctant to get in but couldn't think of a suitable excuse, having agreed to it earlier. She climbed up into the passenger seat in silence. Diggory kept his eyes on her as he circled around the bonnet and got in on the driver's side. There was a slam of the metal door and an instant roar of the V8 engine. Maya noticed that Diggory hadn't bothered with the seatbelt, but she was glad of hers as she jumped and jerked around in her seat as they bounced off the rutted surface of the road. Diggory didn't look at her. His eyes were firmly fixed ahead and his shoulders hunched.

He seemed to be driving away from the village along the high road. They took a sudden lurch down another lane across open farmland, through a small hamlet on the edge of a desolate looking copse and down a green farm track. Why was he going this way? Surely it was away from the village. It was certainly sheltered from the coastline, more secluded, more remote. No-one had been here for a long time and there probably wouldn't be anyone else here for a long time.

Maya looked around. They were going slower now to avoid some of the bigger ruts and muddy brown water filled holes. Maya began to wonder how easy it would be to get out of the Land Rover while it was still moving. Not hard, but the problem was the high banks and hedges either side of the sunken lane. She would have nowhere to go and couldn't possibly climb out of the deep muddy lane before Diggory could be out of the door and drag her back down by the ankles. It's a shame he hadn't put his seatbelt on. It would have given her a few extra seconds. 'No, don't be silly,' she told herself.

The lane seemed to be dropping in height now and twisting back towards the coast. Surely they couldn't be far from the village. Diggory stopped the vehicle where the track become too narrow to go any further. He leant across her. His flushed, reddened, face was directly in front of hers. His stale breath blew warmly on her throat. Maya couldn't help making a sharp intake of breath. Diggory put his hand on the door handle on her side and said, 'It's a bit stiff. You have to have the knack. Here you go,' as the door opened, 'it's just down there past the water works.'

She got out. Her legs were slightly wobbly as she walked off without looking back.

4. A Knave for a Nave

At the garden Guy and Bob were making good progress...in their minds. They now had a good idea what the sequence of construction was going to be and had made sure there was a well-tested supply of sweet hot tea.

A few of the neighbours had leant over the garden wall, as the materials began to stack up, trying to see what was going on. This tended to alternately annoy or amuse Bob, depending on his mood. He wanted to know what was so fascinating about two blokes standing in a garden. Most onlookers didn't speak, even though, for special cases of curiosity, Bob would delight in crossing his eyes, drooping one lip and begin to drool or make inarticulate grunts. He would then adopt a circular motion with one of his legs whilst bending hunchbacked and appear to balance bricks or planks precariously. His behaviour would become increasingly eccentric until either the onlookers were embarrassed, or Guy would distract Bob with another cup of tea; and so they would lose interest, assuming the entertainment was temporarily over.

One nosy neighbour, walking up the lane, stopped in his tracks and wouldn't shift for several minutes. No matter how demented Bob's behaviour became the dark-overcoated, fifty-something, gentleman, with his square heavy framed glasses, just stood and stared. Bob started scratching his groin and then raising one leg like a dog at a lamppost and making theatrical farting noises. He even pretended to try and light one with a match, and burnt his hand in the process, but still the onlooker was completely motionless. In exasperation Bob went over to talk to him.

'Not seen people before then?'

'What?'

'I just wondered if you'd beamed down from another planet to study that very rare human species known as Horticulturas Landscapus?'

'I don't understand.'

'Haven't mastered the language yet then either?'

Guy intervened, 'Stop baiting the poor man. You just don't realise how deeply fascinating you are Bob.'

'Actually I was wondering how far you were going to dig? I'm the local vicar.'

Bob struggled to make a connection, 'Oh I don't think we'll quite get through to the graveyard if that's what you're worried about. But if I strike bone I'll be sure to call you across to read the last rites.'

'No, it's the allotment behind you. I have some carrots and they're very sensitive to root disturbance – well, they are roots, you know. So I'd appreciate it if you didn't dig on that side of the garden until after a week on Saturday.'

Guy said, 'I can't do that. Sorry. We have a schedule to meet, and besides, we can't possibly damage your carrots unless somehow we caused a major land slippage.'

'That may be easier than you think. No, on reflection, I don't think you should be digging.'

Bob: 'Even if I were to throw my spade over the wall like a javelin I can't possibly see how it would do any damage to your carrots.'

'No you mustn't. I won't let you. You don't know. It's awful.'

The vicar's eyes seemed to redden and cloud over. As if to conceal his rage he turned on his heels and with a swish and twirl of his long black coat he was gone, marching and stomping, down the lane.

Bob and Guy had no time to dwell on the conversation as Maya returned. She told them of her walk and her slightly intimidating experience with the farmer.

'I felt so foolish', she said, 'firstly for trusting him, then for not trusting him.'

Guy and Bob had the opportunity, now, to show a more sensitive side of their nature than they had shown to the vicar. They drew the story out from her slowly and without comment. She clearly wanted to tell them, but only if they didn't laugh at her feeling vulnerable. Guy and Bob were the nearest she had to any family or friends in this place. It wasn't very near, as far as she was concerned, but it would have to do. Fortunately they just gave her good practical advice and the reassurance of company and sympathy. It wasn't her fault she felt like that or had got into that situation. Why should half of the population be afraid, or even have to think twice, about walking out on their own or accepting a lift? Bob gave her his mobile phone and asked her to keep it with her for the duration of the job. She could then call Guy, the police or whoever she needed to, at any time. Maya was grateful for it. Not particularly as a practical help, because she wasn't convinced anyone would be able to get to her quickly in a genuine emergency. But she appreciated it as a token of concern and friendship.

She put the phone in her pocket and turned it over continually between her palm and her fingers, as if it was a worry bead to remind her she was not alone. The phone's keys weren't locked and it wasn't long before she was inadvertently accessing the phone settings and setting off the ringtone. She pulled it out of her pocket. It was Wagner's 'Ride of the Valkyries' complete with helmeted opera singers in a flashing animated logo. Guy groaned and Bob looked embarrassed. A broad smile, for the first time in a few hours, spread over Maya's face.

They worked hard from that point on preparing and levelling the ground. They piled some of the heavier obstructions and existing flagstones to one side and the second day ended with the three companions tired but satisfied that they had each, severally and collectively, achieved their goals. After securing their longer term accommodation (they had found a better and nearer Bed and Breakfast than the one recommended by the Tourist Board) and having had much needed showers the three collected on the headland, pints in hand, to watch the spectacular sunset over the miles and miles of sea. Guy thanked the two others for their help during the day although, in truth, Maya had contributed less than Bob. Bob was largely organising and planning the sequence of hard landscape tasks they would be undertaking over the next few days. Maya did her fair share of lifting and carrying a range of materials onto and off site but was happy to follow instructions from the other two. It was as if her body was there but her mind was elsewhere.

Despite the noise of the gulls, and an occasional gust from the coastal breezes, there was a quiet calm to this point in the evening. As they stared out silently towards the horizon Maya's thoughts turned back to the enigmatic figure of St. Endelienta. She tried to visualise what she might have looked like. Maya imagined her in a dark brown cloak covering her almost from head to toe like a shroud. Underneath the rough cloth she could see a slim, small figure with wisps of long ginger hair and a pale freckly face with pale almost non-existent eyebrows glimpsed briefly through the oval opening in her hood. In this dreamlike landscape she drifted, as if without feet, up the wet, grassy, inland valleys from farm to farm fearlessly spreading the word of a mysterious new underground, subversive and exciting cult called …Christianity. A new religion based on a single powerful figure that spoke of kindness not fear. This wasn't the terrifying animal and celestial gods that demanded constant propitiation and hard won sacrifice. This one spread love – pure and simple. The suffering was over. The sacrifice had already been made. Once and for all time there was a new way of living and helping each other. It must have sounded crazy at the time. It still does even in its Twenty First Century establishment dotage. But at this time it was the latest craze – an exciting new fashion from the Middle East, a 'must have' accessory for the thinking man's farmer. The open minded Celts, with their long history of absorbing new ideas from across the sea and making them their own, must have embraced it.

Guy asked her what she was thinking and she mentioned her discovery of the Dark Ages origins of this early saint although she had no facts, merely questions about who Endelienta was and what kind of life she might have led. Guy and Bob had not heard the name before. They were interested but could not really answer or add anything. Talking of the church reminded Bob of his encounter with the vicar. Bob said that he couldn't imagine that this vicar, or priest, or whatever he was, would know anything about Endelienta. Maya thought that this was a little unkind as most vicars in rural communities would have several churches to look after and would be bound to know the stories and legends relating to the area whatever faction or sub-group of the church he represented.

Yawning and now a little chilly, Guy and Maya headed off back to the Bed and Breakfast. Bob wanted to do further research on the local hostelries and, as a slim excuse, promised Maya that he would ask at the bar after the vicar's name and address.

Bob did ask at the Crow's Nest at the top of the village, and he also talked. Bob could hold his liquor better than most but he liked a bit of a gossip when he was drinking and if he didn't know a good story he would probably be just as happy to make one up just to see what reaction he could get. Encouraged by his ability to absorb and exaggerate anything he was told, Bob elicited all kinds of tall fishermen's tales. He also learned a few things about Johnny, the madcap behaviour of foolish tourists (of which he was considered to be one) and more than he really wanted to know about the vicar.

The vicar's name was Henry Ryol (although people locally called him Harry). He was a widower who had lost his wife before he came to the village. He had a house on Fore Street opposite the church. It wasn't a vicarage – just an ordinary terraced house. He ran a local choir in which he would admit no girls no matter how hard their parents pleaded. He had a reputation for being "a bit High Church" and for upsetting some key members of the congregation and Church Wardens. He was a keen committee member of the local Horticultural Society and there was an annual show coming up. There was some bad feeling between the vicar and another member of the Horticultural Society committee – someone called Eskar Pronter. Some said that the rivalry was so intense amongst the vegetable classes that sooner or later there would be bloodshed. They said that Eskar had had some dealings before with the same vicar in another Parish. Eskar was well known as a committed atheist and troublemaker – in fact some said he was a High Priest in the Occult.

To Bob this didn't make much sense: 'surely anyone who believed in the Devil would be soft enough to believe in God as well', he asked.

His informants, who consisted of a couple of old soaks propping up the bar, the landlady and a young couple, exchanged knowing glances. There was also a furtive weasel faced man, with curly dark hair, by the balcony who quickly finished his pint and brushed into Bob impatiently to get to the door and left. 'Who was that?' Bob asked. 'Must be a fire.'

'Name's Penjerrick. I'd steer clear of him if I were you.' Said the Landlord who had just come down the stairs and was lifting the counter and taking his place behind the bar.

'Why?'

'He hates people...and animals...and emmets, sorry tourists...and witches, not necessarily in that order. I tolerate him drinking here because I promised his Dad on his deathbed that I'd keep an eye on him, otherwise I'd have barred him by now. Drog Goes (bad blood). But you were asking about the pagans. Lilly's the expert on that. Her mum's really into that stuff.'

Apparently, Lilly told Bob, there is a lot of Witchcraft about in remote rural communities in the South West and you don't have to believe in the Christian version of the Devil or Satan. They described it as 'the old religion' which was pre-Christian and more in tune with nature and natural sprits.

'There are occult book and gift shops, even a Witchcraft Museum just along the coast in Boscastle.'

'All harmless fun though.'

'Just White Witches.'

Bob asked the difference between a white witch and what he assumed was called a black witch. No-one seemed to know except a white witch tended to admit to it and people knew them and liked most of them. The dark witches, on the other hand, were secretive like the Masons and would pretend to be white witches or not admit to anything.

Lilly, at the bar, suggested that the white witches were basically nice people that believed in a lot of ancient and mysterious pagan forces.
'My mum's not a white witch by the way. Just a pagan, a wiccan. When we were growing up she would explain the real stories behind things like Christmas Trees, Santa Claus, Easter Eggs and so on. These were all pre-Christian.'

There was then some debate about whether astrology was part of it, or different, and whether Tarot Cards were used. Lilly said that she had a friend called Ursell who used them and was really into that sort of thing. In fact she had stopped working at the Golden Lion and got a job in Boscastle so that she could be closer to the Witchcraft Museum and do some research.

'As far as I'm concerned these old stories and myths are just part of our cultural heritage that people come to see', Lilly said, 'which is why it has always been popular in remote tourist spots like North Cornwall or the New Forest. Part of "ye olde England" or in this case "an koth Kernow".'

Bill, who turned out to be one the local crab Fisherman, said he thought 'they were all barking mad. Some were harmless barking mad and some were dangerous barking mad. That's the only difference between the so-called white witches and the rest of them.'

He then rolled his eyes in a disturbing sort of way and said that the white witches had little ceremonies now and then but didn't indulge in the sort of crazed blood soaked orgies of the dark witches. He told Bob of the local gossip that there was some kind of lurid ceremony performed naked on the clifftops during the summer solstice involving the sacrifice of a large cat – some said a Puma, some said a Tiger, some said the legendary Beast of Bodmin. At this point even the credulous Bob realised he was being made fun of and fed a load of tourist tosh; so decided to drink up and call it a day.

It was a clear night as he strode up the hill in a determined zigzag pattern. But he was soon pausing to catch his breath up the hill which was noticeably steeper than when he came down it. Looking back along the narrow street, he could see a bright, white, full moon emerging over the hill from behind the tops of the houses. He was tempted to let out a werewolf's full throated howl but thought it might be anti-social. Even Bob occasionally had limits. Although, if he had noticed the thin lace curtain in the house to his right had started to twitch, and a nervous or curious old lady was looking out, he may well have been tempted to treat her to some devilment. Besides…he was tired, dog tired. He swivelled 240 degrees on his heels and resumed his meandering way back up to the Bed and Breakfast. There was someone following him slowly up the hill but they must have turned off on one of the narrow passages between houses about halfway up. Nobody could sneak up on you in the bright moonshine and it was a beautiful cloudless and still night.

Bob opened the front door and shut it with a bang, made muttered apologies to his silent sleeping hosts, peed in his bedroom sink (the en suite toilet was too low – it must have been plumbed by dwarves he declared to nobody in particular) and started to fall asleep fully clothed on or near his bed. Outside he heard what sounded like the wind starting to pick up or maybe it was a couple of domestic cats that didn't like each other, or a bunch of grown people pretending to be demented banshees. In any case Bob was oblivious within seconds and snoring fit to warp the floorboards.

5. Derring-do with the Famous Five

It was a clear cool morning, although if you looked out to sea there was a hint of mist and haze on the far distant horizon where a container ship moved imperceptibly slowly from right to left like a swan gliding in extreme slow motion. A pair of fishermen or holiday makers were rounding the point of the headland in a small boat. In comparison they seemed to be racing along with a roaring whine of acceleration and the faint acrid puff of cheap diesel.
Maya and Guy were onto the site early. Guy was tempted to give a Bob a "morning call" with an antique hunting horn hanging on the wall of the Bed and Breakfast but Maya gave him one of those "Grow up you little boy" looks and the moment passed.

Bob did turn up after 35 minutes and looking none the worse for wear. He was either not the sort to get a hangover or, more likely, would never admit to having one. As usual he was chipper and cheerful and threw himself straight into sorting out the alignment and levelling of the low timber structure which Guy had christened the "Breakwater". This was a snaking set of low timber posts tied together with thick swags of rope. Unfortunately not all the ordered wood had turned up – the order, and the delivery note, were for twice the amount. Guy rung the supplier who was adamant the shipment had been checked. Johnny Stern had signed the delivery note and closer questioning didn't resolve the discrepancy. 'Probably half-inched', he ventured, 'bunch of wreckers round here. It's in the blood.' Marjorie added that she had seen a couple of lads and Harry the vicar looking at the pile of wood but not seen anything suspicious.

After a hard morning's work the work was as finished as it could be with the material available but Bob wasn't satisfied. Guy asked him what was wrong and he explained that the basic structure was okay but now that he saw it on site he felt it lacked character. He likened it to a picket fence and said that it needed roughing up a bit. Guy suggested distressing some of the timbers with a chainsaw. This unwarranted vandalism upset Bob who was loath to ruin good wood.

Then it occurred to Bob that what he needed was additional wood that was already distressed. He felt that what the design lacked was some genuinely random driftwood. He could build this out at right angles to the main structure with a few isolated posts like disused and abandoned groins such as the ones that he had seen on some beaches in other parts of the country. These were used to retain the sand or shingle before finally being washed and eroded into ineffective and isolated posts by the continual beating of the sea and the shells and stones that it carried before it. Guy liked the idea but cautioned Bob that it would take him a long time to find the kind of material he wanted. He told him that he would be more likely to find plastic rubbish than timber washed ashore but he was welcome to see what he could find. The randomness of it also appealed to both of them as they were both great believers in incorporating random and interesting objects into the design found locally. Guy had occasionally dug up previously thrown away objects like clay pots and tree stumps and made new features of them in the gardens he was improving. He was not the sort of precious designer who insisted on a plan being carried out without variation. He preferred people to contribute to the creative process as the garden took shape. Even, God forbid, on occasion, taking a good idea from the client.

So Bob set out on the coast path rising from the harbour behind the fish sheds. He walked for about a quarter of an hour feeling the fresh North Atlantic wind blow away his jaded "morning after the night before" feel until he came across his first bay to explore. Dropping and slipping over the wet granite along the line of a freshwater stream, as it tumbled down to the shore, Bob felt as if he were completely alone. All the traffic and noise of the harbour were a world away. Behind him was Lobber Point, a gorse covered hill studded with yellow flowers that smelled curiously of coconut. They say "when the gorse is not in flower there is no love to be had". Just as well there is almost always the odd bloom out. Where he had just left the stream Yellow Iris was paddling in the fresh water, but in front of him was just rock and ocean. The sea was a luminescent Mediterranean greenish-blue under a clear powder blue sky. Bob could make out the impressive outline of Tintagel further up the coast. Far better to see it from this distance than be in it, thought Bob, who was not too impressed with the endless King Arthur trinkets on sale. He described it to Maya as 'a stunning rocky outcrop crowned by mysterious monastic ruins and surrounded by shops of unremitting squalor and tat.' It was always all or nothing with Bob. He called a spade a shovel and was not too proud to offend anyone who was silly enough to be precious or sensitive.

Having mentally satisfied himself of his good judgement and taste Bob took to scouring the rocky pools and crevices for interesting trophies. When Bob, Guy and Maya had gone through Port Gaverne at low tide he had seen lots of weed entwined bits and pieces and so he was slightly surprised when after 20 or so minutes happy truffle hunting he hadn't found a single artefact. There were some interesting rocks he would have liked, if he could have carried them, but he suspected they looked rather better where they were, than lifted into a suburban garden. He didn't even find the plastic flotsam and jetsam that Guy had promised. Still, he enjoyed himself looking and jumping and splashing about. The seaside kid in him was delighted just to look. If he had found a bucket and spade (and there had been any sand on the rocky shore) he doubtless would be digging the moat on his sandcastle by now.

He thought he saw some driftwood, washing in a pool under the cliffs to the extreme left of the bay, where the deep shadow from overhanging cliffs made the water appear oily and black. He climbed over the rocks and gingerly clambered around a few other water filled crevices. But as soon as he climbed over the last rock he saw immediately that it wasn't the smooth bleached wood he had hoped for but was a thick, off-white, belt. He bent down to pick it up. It was leather but was no longer flexible. It seemed to have become stiff with dried salt and this had obliterated whatever colour it may have originally been. Probably pale brown. Bob threw it back in. He looked around under the base of the cliff but all he could find was a few discarded needles and some rusting old cans.

Just then he noticed he was not alone on the beach. There was someone in the distance dragging something large, dark and shiny like a seal, but it could just as easily have been a body bag or a heavyweight black net. Rounding the headland there was a boat with two other men. The man on the beach called out to the two men something like 'Billy!' or 'Bully!' and the boat turned around and headed back where it had come from. After a while he decided to walk on up the coast path to find the next bay. He climbed up the steep earthen steps through the gorse, around a stone wall and down the next slope. But here there was no way down. The fields just dropped away into steep cliffs. Bob was tempted to climb, fancying himself as a bit of a mountaineer, but even he realised it was probably too dangerous. Nonetheless he enjoyed teetering on the edge and trying to see what the shoreline was like. Then he noticed a small falcon flying along the cliff edge. He strained his eyes to try and make out what type it might be, but he was looking into the sun and it just looked like a black arrowhead. Too slow for a Peregrine; a Merlin perhaps, he thought, as he twisted around to follow its flight and almost slipped on the wet grass.

He walked on for another ten minutes without seeing an obvious way down. The larks were singing inland, drowned out, as the wind swirled, by the occasional screech of the gulls and seabirds. There was a stiff onshore breeze (when was there not?) and, today, it kept the clouds away. At last he saw another possible cleft in the green sloping fields that he was approaching. He stepped over a wooden style through a stone wall and into the field. To one side, set against the wall, was a little stone roof over what appeared to be a natural spring or well. Above it was an ancient gnarled thorn tree in which someone had tied little ribbons and hung small mirrors and beads intertwined with miniature arrangements of native flowers. Bob looked at this for a while wondering what the significance might be. In the grass around the site was a narrow worn groove where many boots had trod over the years but Bob stepped off this and followed the bank in the direction of the sea. There were a few, low, wind-blown gorse bushes to negotiate and then the ground seemed to slope suddenly away to the sea. Perhaps there was just a smaller cliff at the end of it. Small, but still deadly if you slipped. He looked up and down the bank to see if there was a sensible way down. He tried walking in both directions but to either side the ground just seemed to stop in mid-air. Disappointed, he decided to head back up the steep bank. Impatient to get back up to the level of the path he was almost half running, half scrambling his way back up through the grassy hummocks and bushes. He suddenly felt the ground give way beneath his left foot. Instinctively, he grabbed out with his right hand and tried to hold onto something. He managed to get hold of a thin old woody stem of twining clematis, that didn't have the sharp thorns of the gorse, but it wasn't enough to hold his weight. His right foot followed his left into the hole opening up beneath him as the ground gave way. All that clutching onto the twine did was to twist and swing him around Tarzan-like, smashing his stomach into a large rock which had been concealed in the undergrowth. This winded him badly but worse was to come. He was still moving and as he slowly slid back from the rock he fell fully into the blackness of a deep hole.

The first thing he felt was relief. It had seemed a long drop but he had been surprised and grateful that it wasn't the eighty foot or so down to sea level. He was also surprised that his landing was soft. He would have expected cold, wet, rock, dripping with icy ground water. Then he was surprised by the pain. Both ankles, both knees, both elbows and the side of his head. Then he felt the real pain. A sharp, penetrating, stabbing pain in his right wrist. He tried to feel his fingers. He could move them but they felt curiously cold and numb.

He peered into the gloom but his eyes were slow to adjust to the darkness. He had no way of telling whether he was down a shaft the size of a well or a football stadium. All he could see was the narrow shaft of light above him taunting him with a glimmer of fresh air, sky and the sound of crashing waves and crying seagulls.

Eventually he could see a little more of the earth and rock within a circumference of, maybe, a couple of feet around him. His chest and shoulders were dimly illuminated at the bottom of the narrow shaft of light. Around the edge of the most visible rock he could see a very pale stone surface. He thought at first it was chalk and then he realised this was impossible. He must be hundreds of miles from the nearest chalk cliff. Perhaps it was a milky Quartz. He felt his clothes becoming wet and filthy from the bottom of his cage-like hole. He tried to move and the rasping of his dragging boots within the cave seemed to echo unbearably loud. For a second he felt compelled to yell for help. But no sooner had he loosed his first salvo than he regretted it. There was probably no-one within a mile radius to help him. Nonetheless he listened and he thought he could hear a low grumbling sound.

He tried to move his legs upright. His feet seemed to be burning up with friction inside his socks and were sore from the fact that his new boots were slightly too large for him and he felt his heel and toes aching from where they had been banging from his walk and climb. From the ankle up he could feel his leg muscles taut and strained. They seemed to tighten rather than move at his command. Nonetheless he swung his right leg over his left making his torso rotate like a stuck beetle on the harder ground to his side. He couldn't detect much wrong except that the effort wasn't moving him upwards so he twisted his pelvis and stamped his right foot on the ground to gain some leverage. He flapped his arms out to find something to pull or lean on but there was nothing. By continuing to move his arms and shoulders though he set up a rather ungainly rocking, early prototype helicopter-like action which gave him enough momentum to pull himself up off his left leg. With relief he realised that neither of his legs were broken, although his left leg wouldn't properly take his weight. He gingerly felt a massive bruise on his left thigh where, in his schooldays he had learnt the hard way, was a good place to give someone a 'dead leg'.

He hobbled in the direction of the lighter rock surface as it was the only thing he could see to lean against. Bob wasn't the type to panic lightly, or feel claustrophobic, but even he felt a sickening hollow stomach and dry throat from the shock now that he was upright. There was trickle of wet cold sweat running down his spine under his lumberjack shirt. His nostrils burned with the acrid smell of … what was it? It was like some chemical or acid. Then he recognised it. It was urine. Strong burning urine. Not me, he thought, even I don't usually smell that bad. He looked suspiciously at the dirt smearing his hand and raised it to his face to smell it when he felt a thump from behind and was knocked to the ground. He felt a tearing and cutting on his lower leg but fortunately the bulk of the blow was blunted on the underside of his boots. Suddenly Bob felt a lot more agile than he had done a few seconds earlier and propelled, as if on a trampoline, he started to climb up the lighter rock he had seen. There must have been a few footholds or cracks to get his boots into and further up there was a bit of vegetation or fern to grip onto using one of his hands. Without looking back Bob climbed up and could see that the rock was not pale because of whatever geological substance it was composed of, but lit by a greenish-white light from another entrance. There seemed to be a roughly horizontal shaft above the lower cave and he was able to crawl up this in the direction of the light. He couldn't hear anything behind him as he was deafened by the beat of his own heart and the pumping of blood in his cranium. As it became brighter he scrambled through the roots of some tussocky grass and then, suddenly, out into the sweet cold air. He collapsed onto his back on the grassy bank and felt absolutely safe. Whatever, or whoever, it was that attacked him he could surely deal with it now he was back on even terms in a daylight world he could recognise.

Minutes passed and whatever adrenalin had previously given him courage now seemed to have drained completely. He began to feel tired and cold and sick again. If he was going to move, he had to go now. No matter how slowly, he needed to try and get back to Port Isaac. He tried to lean on his wrist, to get up, but it collapsed painfully under his weight. His vision blacked out and he felt a swirling sickness in his stomach from the pain in his wrist. He could hear, but none of his other senses seemed to function as fully as he expected. His body seemed to be cutting down on the non-essential. Bob just had to hope he was going to stay conscious. He stayed still for a few more minutes, gathering his breath and setting himself some meaningless and fairly simple arithmetic calculations to keep his mind ticking over. But he soon got bored with that and let his mind drift into a numb blankness. Eventually the pain began to subside into more of a deadening ache. He felt less dizzy and a little stronger. Using his other wrist to lever himself up this time, he got to his knees and, eventually, upright. Taking a deep draft of fresh ocean breath, he set off grimly back to the coast path. At first he rested every ten or twelve steps, and then less often, as his body began to obey his command to perform a monotonous blank robotic stumble back to civilisation.

Eventually he returned over the brow of the hill and caught sight of the Port. This stirred him on until he saw a bench on the path overlooking the harbour. The temptation to sit was just too great for Bob. He fell onto it, curled up like a tramp, and lost consciousness.

6. Exeter Stage Left

The afternoon was getting late and Guy needed some advice from Bob on the footings for a small platform. After Maya got fed up of Guy moaning about Bob sloping off to the seaside she gently suggested that he went and got him. Guy agreed to go as far as the start of the path at the top of the village and no further. He looked out but could not see around the path so he walked slowly around the front of the last houses and up to the start of open pasture. He couldn't see anyone coming along the path. He stood staring into the lowering sun for a few minutes and decided to turn back.

As he swung around he thought he saw something flapping in the breeze above a wooden bench. Was it a coat someone had left? He looked again and took a few steps to a higher point to get a better view. It was part of Bob's shirt that was waving at him. It must have been torn or just become unbuttoned but Guy knew at once that something more than that was wrong. There was something ugly and unnatural in Bob's twisted posture that suggested more than excessive relaxation.

Guy called out as he sprang up the remaining part of the sloping steps towards the bench. There was no response. He called again and by that time was standing looking over him. He couldn't take his eyes off Bob's hand which seemed to dangle at the wrong angle for his arm. Bob meanwhile was drifting back into to consciousness stimulated by the sound of Guy's voice and from the needling discomfort of pain. He groaned, cleared his throat and spoke, 'I think I've broken my arm and I'm not sure about my ankle. Just sprained I guess. Can you give me a hand?'

'No, I need both of mine' said Guy but felt his joke dry up in his throat and got on with the awkward business of helping Bob up onto his feet, then slowly and awkwardly through the stile gate and gingerly down the earth steps onto the footpath. Once at the top of the tarmac road Guy left his friend leaning on some railings while he went to fetch Bob's truck and Maya. It was a tight squeeze getting past some of the parked cars and he managed to leave some white paint on the corner of the Fish Cellars' wall but he was fairly quickly back with Maya to load Bob into the cab.

'You any idea where to take me?'

'None at all. There must be a casualty place somewhere. Maya – can you ask someone as we pass through the harbour?'

Maya duly did. She didn't speak to Bob. Neither of them did. They just concentrated on the task in hand, as if Bob was a sack of potatoes or a corpse.

'I think there's a surgery near the school at the top of New Road.'

After a second asking they managed to find it.

It was closed.

'Don't people get ill around here?' asked an exasperated Bob.

They returned down New Road to the nearest shop and asked again. A helpful lady patiently explained the joys of rural healthcare. The options seemed to be to call an NHS 111 health-line who might put them through to a duty doctor (but they were advised that he in turn was only likely to refer them to a hospital for X-Ray), to find a Cottage Hospital in a town 40 miles away that might or might not provide emergency care or travel 70 miles, in a different direction, to Exeter where they would be sure of finding a properly equipped Casualty Department. They opted for the latter. After all, they reasoned, if they had to call an ambulance it would presumably have to make the trip both ways. Quicker to drive themselves. 'Good job I haven't had a heart attack or half-drowned in the sea, you'd have to ask for a helicopter' muttered Bob who was clearly going to make a grumpy patient.

It was fairly slow drive through to the next County's Casualty unit and then a frustratingly long time in the Minor Injuries Unit. Despite it still being early in the evening there had already been a couple of possible head injuries from a bar room brawl and someone cut out from a serious Road Traffic Accident that took priority in A&E. Bob was then sent down to the X-Ray unit where Bob couldn't have been looked after better. He expected to be sent home with what he had been told was a minor injury but because of the fall and some corresponding bruising to the head the Doctor overruled the earlier assessment and wanted to keep him in overnight for observation. They allocated him a bed which turned out to be in a private room in an isolation ward. A matter of chance he was told by a nice Cornish lady called Ursell. They apparently didn't have any highly contagious or disruptive individuals to put on that ward so Bob was the next best thing!

Whilst he was settling in and asking if there were any hospital pyjamas he could borrow Ursell came in with the confirmation that he did have a hairline fracture but it was quite faint and wouldn't need a cast but he did need to restrict movement for a while. How long would he have to take off work? No time at all, he was told, providing he could do it with one hand. But he was advised he might have a bit of a struggle getting dressed and undressed. Did he have a wife, girlfriend or partner that could help him? 'Only a business partner, at least in this neck of the woods', he replied.

When his hospital duty pyjamas arrived and another attractive young nurse called Maga volunteered to help him change Guy and Maya wandered off to the local late opening Supermarket to get some grapes and a few sandwiches for themselves. Guy even toyed with the idea of a Get Well Soon card but couldn't find one suitably abusive or robust enough in its humour.

When they got back to the Ward Bob had already relaxed and looked a great deal more tired and ill than he had previously. Maga advised that he should probably get some rest. So, in that age old hospital tradition, the visitors sat and ate their victim's grapes completely ignoring the person they had come to visit. They had been so wrapped up in the business of just dealing with the consequences that it had not really occurred to them until now to consider what had happened to Bob and why. Maya picked up one of Bob's shoes to examine the deep lacerations that would otherwise have been made to his feet. They considered again the sounds and the smells Bob had described. Was it a feral cat defending its young? Was it something bigger – a black jaguar like the so called Beast of Bodmin? Or was it just some demented Black Backed or

Herring Gull? Guy had seen how aggressive and noisy these birds were, particularly when they had young. He particularly despised the large Herring Gulls which made the small Black Headed Gulls that appeared on the South Coast near to where he lived seem so polite and well-behaved. The Herring Gulls delighted in aiming their excrement at him and any vehicle he happened to have. This wouldn't be quite so bad if it could be washed off easily. Unfortunately it had the consistency of quick drying concrete and, once set, had to be chipped off taking with it chunks of whatever it was attached to. He quite liked the small elegant Fulmars, although he had even been spat on once by them when he had strayed near one's nest.

They wondered if the hole that Bob had fallen into might be some sort of smuggler's cave. Maya dismissed this as a foolish romantic notion. Guy described an incident which had occurred that year of a wrecked ship which had come to grief in stormy weather on the Cornish coast. It had made national headlines because of the speed, organisation and enthusiasm with which the local population had rushed onto the rocks to take away thousands of tons of timber and other assorted goods. These were the direct descendants of the wreckers and no passing of a few generations was going to change their positive attitude to what they considered their birth right – the fruits of the sea.

Guy also reminded Maya about the eccentric behaviour of Harry the local vicar. Why had he been so keen that they shouldn't dig down too deep within Johnny's garden? Was there some sort of cave under the garden as well? Was Harry like the vicar of the smuggling tales surrounding Jamaica Inn up on the moor? When Guy had enquired about any surveys that Johnny may have had done prior to purchasing the house he had mentioned that mines went under most of Cornwall, never mind this village. There was supposed to be several entrances including one from the sea cliff on the other side of the huge concrete breakwaters. There was a possibility that they ran directly under the garden but Johnny had rushed into buying the house without commissioning the proper mining survey that the building surveyor and Estate Agent had both recommended.

Maya recounted again her story about the local farmer Diggory who had been so charming and then suddenly become so threatening. She hadn't said too much about her feelings of fear and helplessness before – she had just described how foolish and naive she felt. Guy put his arm around her and Bob, who had appeared to have been dozing, held out his good hand to hold hers. Maya was reassured that at least she had two good friends. She also felt secure that they were friends – they were not about to take advantage of her in any sense except the purely professional. In other words making her work hard by planting and digging and doing her job as well as or better than them. That was fine by her. She wanted to be one of the lads - horticulturally anyway.

'Was there no-one else at the farm? No-one working out in the fields?' Guy asked.

'No. I thought I heard someone but I never saw anyone. I guess it could have been an animal.'

There was a pause. Then she continued. 'He made great play of shouting to someone but I'm beginning to wonder now if that was all an act because when I went into the kitchen there was no evidence that he didn't live alone. Now I come to think of it there were only dirty or washed dishes enough for one person. There was something in the décor that said "wife" or "mother" to me though.'

'What? Pink frilly curtains?'

'No. It was just there were a range of diagonally hung ornamental pans and a few pictures. Nothing really conclusive – it just looked decorated and I don't think a busy bachelor farmer would have bothered with anything that wasn't strictly functional. He didn't look the type to be a whiz in the kitchen and forever holding dinner parties. I think there had been someone else sharing that kitchen but that she hadn't been around for a while.'

'Could be a he?'

'No. Not the way he looked at me. He was charming and said all the right things but there was something right from the moment he first saw me. What's that expression – mentally undressing me with his eyes?'

'Well why didn't you scarper straight away?'

Maya shifted her eyes away from direct contact with Guy and said very quietly, 'Because I was doing it to him before he was doing it to me. Anyway', she quickly continued,' he was perfectly civil the first time around. It was only when I got back from St. Endellion that he was like a different person. It was as if I had come at the wrong time and was in danger of discovering something or someone he didn't want me to see. I think he has some secret, some awful secret that he's ashamed of. I definitely got the impression that he was on the edge of violence. I just misunderstood why, in what way and probably who might have been on the receiving end.'

Maya looked up as if she had been talking to herself and only just realised that Guy and Bob were there. Guy made a sort of 'hmmm' noise and Bob nodded gently and slipped off to sleep deeply this time. There was a period of silence followed by some renewed slurping of grapes. It was clear this was all they were going to get to eat tonight and both of them were determined not to go hungry; the sandwiches they had earlier had barely touched the sides. One of the side effects of manual labour in fresh air is a healthy appetite and a raging thirst, when combined with shock and boredom it has the potential to become an obsessive compulsion.

To distract his stomach Guy started to muse aloud about Johnny. Maya had not really gotten to know him yet and he had barely spoken a word to Bob. Keeping the client happy was Guy's job and he was welcome to it. Guy told her, 'you know, just before we came down here they were doing a series of afternoon movies on the telly on the theme of naval warfare. They had that 'Master and Commander' and something that was a bit like 'Pirates of the Caribbean' only with no jokes, but they also had some classic 40's and 50's films about the Second World War. They also had one on the First World War. I hadn't really realised that there was a lot of sea warfare in the First World War. Anyway Johnny was actually in the First World War one and one of the Second World War ones. Funnily enough the one about the First World War was the later of the two and was shot in colour but I guess the other one was made shortly after or even during the war. In both of them he played a stiff upper lip against all odds sort of hero. The interesting thing I found about it was that he wasn't acting.'

'What do you mean?'

'I mean just that. You know some actors are like chameleons. They take on all kinds of voices, different appearances and in real life they are just bland or play another role – that of film star celebrity chat show guest with their little anecdotes and scripted stories. Well Johnny was just Johnny. He was exactly the same person in both of those films as in real life. The same voice, the same mannerisms, the same dialogue almost. Of course he was half a century younger but that was all. It was if he had been frozen in time. Frozen in that character. What I'd like to know is: which was the chicken and which was the egg?'

'I always assumed that actors who don't change from film to film, that always play the same sort of character, are just following a winning formula. You know FILM 1 then FILM 2 THE SEQUEL and so on. The film industry funding is so conservative they will only fund something that has already made money. So they ask people to repeat a role.'

'I think it went deeper than that, Maya. I think there was something in Johnny's own personality that the film makers picked up on in casting him in those heroic roles. And you know what they say about wartime heroes not wearing well in peace time. He can't adjust to obscurity and living a normal retired life.'

'But is that any reason to make himself so obnoxious? I get the impression he's not too well liked by anyone that knows him.'

'Perhaps. He has enemies, that's for sure, and we're not talking about people who would just cross the street or go up a different supermarket aisle to avoid talking to him. I mean serious ones who have been convicted for GBH and other offences. I was asking Marjorie who was the best farmer to approach for topsoil and manure. She just gave me a list of people not to go to. One of them was a farmer up the hill. Somewhere near where you must have gone. Marjorie described him as 'a dangerous man'. He and Johnny had got into a fight about some organised dog fighting and illegal hunting. I don't remember the details but Johnny was taking up the cause of animal cruelty and wanted to show the farmer how it felt to be treated like beasts of the field. It got quite nasty. But the weird thing was no-one got prosecuted. It all got hushed up. The farmer has subsequently sworn some sort of revenge and he's not the sort to go to the law to protect himself. Maybe your friend realised who you were working for and that's why his attitude changed. Maybe there was something in the barn to do with that illegal dog fighting or badger baiting or whatever they get up to that he didn't want you to see.'

Maya said, 'I can't believe that's the same farmer. I know I might have misread Diggory but I still felt there was a basic level of gentle kindness in him ... as well, admittedly, as some kind of sadness or secret. I know I said I felt him capable of violence. But it was a kind of righteous indignation or over-protecting a family member or something that was bad for a good reason if you know what I mean. Besides, I wouldn't rush into judging who was right and wrong in any scrapes that Johnny was involved in.'

They both looked out of the ward window towards a rainy and dark car park. A few ornamental trees bent lightly in the wind. The nurses were now changing shift and seemed to glide across the car park in small, cloaked, clumps in both directions as they huddled together deep in fast moving conversation. Beyond the car park the yellowish lights of a nearby office block illuminated the horizon, punctuated with occasional car and lorry headlights.

Guy and Maya were separately wondering where to spend the night. After a few moments they seemed to arrive at the same conclusion. It didn't take more than a few gestures and grunts of agreement to communicate that they didn't want to stay in Exeter and started up Bob's truck for the long journey back to Port Isaac.

When they telephoned the hospital in the morning there had been another change of shifts and nobody was quite sure how Bob was, who Bob was or where Bob was. The Hospital receptionist and Ward sister virtually refused to talk to them as they were not immediate family. Eventually they got a call from Bob to say he had been discharged and could he please be got the hell out.

7. High Speed Death

Bob had been given the all clear to leave but, with his wrist firmly plastered, he had been told in no uncertain terms not to do any manual labour. As this was the time when he should have been laying the foundations of the hard landscaping, he found instead that he had taken on the role of grumpy foreman and giving unnecessarily idiot proof guidance to Guy and Maya. The atmosphere wasn't particularly helped by the return of Johnny and Marjorie. Guy had hoped to be a bit further on by the time they returned but, of course, it wasn't to be. They were a good two days behind, even with the contingencies that Guy had put into the planning. This meant that, instead of having finished the hard landscaping and taking delivery of the first plants, the site was at that World War One stage that all garden makeovers go through. A previously dull but recognisably garden-like area had been stripped into an bald and uninviting building site with materials, tools and rocks piled all over the place in a sea of mud and rubble. Guy couldn't see this: he could only see the vision, of what he wanted, starting to take shape. For the client this was always the lowest ebb – the "why did we do it?" moment. All they could see was that a bunch of strangers had turned up and totally ruined their garden.

Johnny kept coming out to ask Guy question after question. They were mostly details of cost and design elements. Guy's responses were mostly 'Wait and See' or 'All will be revealed' but after the 15th time it was beginning to wear a bit thin for all concerned. Guy was naturally reluctant to commit to advertising effects and small details that he may later want to change. But he did have to commit on cost and swallow the overrun if there was one. Johnny wouldn't accept the normal builder's practice of submitting a bill in excess of the estimate as time and materials overran. They had agreed a fixed price and would not want any slight improvement unless it resulted in a cost reduction. Guy made a mental note to economise on the size of some of the 'filler' and 'windbreak' plants so that he could still realise any design changes he wanted to make on the fly with the 'feature' or 'showstopper' elements. For instance, in one difficult and shady corner of the building, near a services manhole he was going to place an Emerald and Gold Euonymous. It was a cheap and cheerful solution for all year around colour rather than a spectacular or imaginative choice and so Guy resolved to get a first year rooted cutting rather than a larger 3 or 4 year old plant with instant impact. Guy was not the sort of designer that liked to leave a garden deteriorating as soon as he left it – he couldn't shake the habit of wanting to plant for the future. If this left the clients less instantly gratified then so be it. They would thank rather than curse him in years to come or so he hoped.

But having Bob on his case as well as the client was becoming more than the normally taciturn and placid Guy could reasonably be expected to bear. Suddenly the solution to his problems and the opportunity to get on and try to recover some labour time occurred to him. Maya smiled in recognition as he suggested to Bob that he take Johnny down to the Golden Lion to explain how the hard landscaping element would function in terms of outdoor dining and how the found objects and sculptural ideas would be dramatically lit when Johnny and his wife wanted to entertain guests in the evening. Johnny was not one to refuse a free drink and the opportunity to speak to a captive audience. Bob, to his credit, was not one to refuse the opportunity to buy someone else a drink as long as he could join them.

With a single armful of drawings Bob set off with Johnny for much needed refreshment. The humour of both of them seemed to be immeasurably improved by a more congenial setting.

'At least this doesn't look like a building site', started Johnny, 'mind you they did redecorate this Spring. Closed the bar for 7 days just for a lick of paint. I had to go down to the Slipway.'

'But I thought you liked to drink at the Slipway anyway'.

'I do but that's not the point. I didn't have any choice. Plus the Slipway don't do High Speed Death.'

'What's that?'

'HSD? High Speed Death. That's what the locals call it. Those from St. Austell call it Hick's Special Draft but I reckon after three pints of it that if you try to drive home you'll know why they call it High Speed Death. The Slipway do a nice Sharps' Doom but HSD is the real stuff. You try it.'

'Well, I'm not driving so I don't mind if I do. What'll you have?'

'Mine's a Glenmorangie. Double please'.

Bob's heart sunk. This was going to be expensive. He wondered if he could claim expenses and resolved to mention the garden at least once to make this a 'business meeting'. As it happened he never did remember and both of them happily chatted away without giving a second thought to the finer points of garden construction.

Johnny launched into one of his tales of derring-do on the High Seas. If there was a reason or a connection to anything else it was so tenuous and fleeting that it passed Bob's notice. He might have said, 'That reminds of the time when...' but he might not. Johnny was a good storyteller. He had certainly had enough practice to fine tune his repertoire and it had become mature and polished. Bob was not above telling a yarn or two himself but he could scarcely get a word in. He tried to ask a few questions though during drinking pauses – there were no pauses for breath.

'Did you ever do any filming off the Cornish coast?'

'Oh yes, but not for war films. Once did a costume drama at Charlestown. They have some tall ships there in the harbour and they made a really good set for press-ganging sailors for a smuggling tale. There were hundreds of empty barrels supposed to be full of brandy. Funnily enough we did some of the interiors and shots of houses up in the North though. We used the Old Post Office at Tintagel for the inside and Roscarrock House just above Port Isaac for the outside. I was against using Roscarrock because I was sure it had been used in that stupid soap they did. What was its name? That bloke Ennis. Some heart throb. Women didn't get out much if they thought he was attractive. Oh God, what's its name? Stupid Doctor in the funny little house at Port Quinn. It'll come to me.'

Bob started to ask him a supplementary question as Johnny suddenly exploded, 'Poldark! Should remember it. I think they even named one of the mines after it ...or perhaps it was always called that. Not that it brings the tourists in anyway. They're not that stupid. Well, not all of them. I suppose they think it's a good place to go if it's raining.'

Bob asked him if there were any mines or quarries near Port Isaac.

Johnny ignored him or misunderstood. He was off on some recollection about smuggling in the film or TV drama that he was remembering and started to talk about smuggler's caves in the area. 'Had a funny experience when we were doing the Roscarrock bit. The film crews were asking the locals if there were any places that could be used for filming a smuggler's cave. They said no of course. What else would they say? Anyway they came across some simple chap who was eager to please. I think he must have long since died or moved on but he used to be a regular in the back room at the Golden Lion where I had that unfortunate encounter with Bully. He said yes, there's hundreds of little caves good enough for hiding contraband and offered to take us to see one. I had been waiting all day for some stupid tart to get her make up sorted out. She only had one line to say but she couldn't seem to get the make up or the hair or something right. Anyway I'd had a nip or two whilst I was bored out my tiny waiting in the Green Room and the Director suggested it would bring an authentic country freshness to my cheeks if I might like to get some fresh air before they filmed my scene. So I offered to go with this rather fetching teenage research assistant while this wizened old yokel took us to find some stupid smuggler's cave. I needn't have bothered. The place was far too steep, damp and slippery to move a heavy camera tripod around. I could hardly keep my winkle pickers under control. In the end they mocked up the scene in a studio in Bristol.'

There was a pause. Bob wondered what had been 'funny' about the experience. Johnny had only paused, as was his custom, to make sure his glass was fully charged before getting around to the nub of any one tale. Bob eventually took the hint, got the round in and normal service was resumed. 'Well, like I say, it was really slippery and the stupid shoes they had fitted me with were too tight. I fell down some gap when I was following them. Lost the buckle on the damned shoe. Anyway they pulled me up to the top of the bank and I sent them back down to find this buckle as it was a genuine antique one. The old man was very reluctant but a stiff jab up his jacksy with my good shoe seemed to encourage him. They were ages grubbing around for it whilst I had to wait. The old man kept muttering but the research skivvy was really getting into it. Probably fancied herself as Dora The Female Explorer. But then she found a skeleton with a ring on its finger. At least that's what she thought it was. Give out a right blood-curdler. The old man ran off. The research assistant came back with the finger bone and the ring that had become fused onto it. Said she was going straight to the police. Turned out to be a monkey paw. She thought it was a child's – the silly mare. Never did find the place again. I went back out there with the police as the girl was under sedation but it all looked the same to me. I couldn't tell one gorse bush from the next. Well you wouldn't would you? Anyway how did you say you got your lucky break?'

Johnny indicated Bob's wrist. Bob must have told him about 3 times already how he had fallen into a hidden mine shaft or hole somewhere off the coastal path but he did so again now because of the resonance with the story Johnny had just told him. Unfortunately Johnny's attention had already wandered. A group of young blondes from London had entered the bar and rather noisily taken up the bar stools in front of Johnny. The giggling high Kensington accents and the bright short skirts ranked in front at eye level were too much for Johnny's attention. He decided in the middle of Bob's sentence to get up from the table and offer the girls a drink. Bob was more astonished by his sudden generosity than his inattentive rudeness. It turned out that one of the girls was a regular summer visitor and had met Johnny before. She introduced the others to Johnny and they became engrossed in their own chatter about the weather, clothes and mutual acquaintances. Johnny seemed to be in his element so Bob finished his drink and quietly slipped out.

Bob walked out across the concrete apron known as the Platt, stepping over the chains that moored the fishing boats and past a few parked cars and onto the beach. He was still stiff and sore but he was glad to be out in the open. There was something soothing about the regular, rhythmic crashing of the small waves on the beach. A gentle swooshing sound that calmed the soul and encouraged you to breathe the fresh salty air deep into the lungs as you felt any knots in your shoulders unravel and untwist in a single relaxed sigh. Bob strolled along the joining line of sand and water and then sat to one side on a handy rock. The combination of fresh air, soothing waves and the HSD lying heavily upon Bob's stomach made him deeply contented. He stared out to sea, thinking nothing more than, 'this is the life!' Even Johnny's abandonment of him didn't disturb him. In fact he was grateful to be on his own. No chatter, no massaging of customer's egos ('after all that's supposed to be Guy's job') and no silly stories or nonsense about caves.

After a while he got up and, with his enormous boots (he never wore shoes), he splashed through the stream running along the south side of the beach. Not that it was deep: the water just spilled out flat across the sand and shingle in a score of little tributaries and runnels. He wandered aimlessly amongst the rockpools looking at different sizes, colours and shapes of seaweed. In doing so he noticed a few small shrimp-like creatures which he at first had mistaken for fish. But he thought he did see the occasional very small dark fish darting out of sight so quickly that all you saw was a fleeting impression of movement and perhaps some sand or seaweed still settling where it had been disturbed.

He thought of childhood memories of the seaside. He thought he could remember dabbling in rock pools but realised that he had been brought up on Weymouth sands without a rock in sight. Perhaps it was a collective folk memory of the Great British seaside. It also brought back uncomfortable memories of his mother and his sister. Plus there was someone missing. He tried to visualise his father and realised he couldn't. He couldn't remember what he looked like. He'd known him as a toddler but he had left the family quite early. Bob scoured the family shelves of his memory trying to remember photographs on mantelpieces or stuck away in dusty black albums. He could remember one image of his father and mother at the seaside. It was just after their marriage, long before they had kids. They were both in beach gear. He remembered because his elder sister used to giggle over it. Fashions had changed a lot and what must have seemed daring and racy at the time looked odd and almost Victorian only ten years later. He remembered his father was holding a huge ice cream cornet up to his face. He couldn't see his face properly in the photograph, just some wispy blond hair blowing in the wind and already thinning. His mother had a striped all-in-one costume. They were horizontal stripes. A bad choice for someone raised on fish and chips. His father was well muscled but any illusion of a Baywatch pinup was destroyed by his enormous shorts that reached down past his knees and terminated in a wide and curiously triangular flare.

The high cotton wool clouds scudded over in a stiff breeze that seemed to be lacking from the shelter of the south side of the

Port. Here an enormous dark rocky hill brooded over the beach – protecting it and threatening it simultaneously. But Bob stood with his back to it – looking out to sea. There was an intense blue brightness at the horizon. He made his way along a ridge between the boulders so that he could see out past the Breakwaters at the entrance. To his right he could just catch a glimpse of the island he recognised as Tintagel Head.

His sister, Melissa, had been taken into care for a couple of years during her teens. She had a nervous breakdown when she was pregnant and her mother forced her to have an abortion. All Bob could remember was the shouting, the crashing of shut doors in his face, the exclusion from his mother (whom he had previously adored) and the horrible feeling that he didn't know what he had done wrong. His father had already left by this time and yet his mother seemed to blame his father, and every male in the street including the young Bob.

Recently, after his mother had died of lung cancer, he made an effort to spend time with his sister. During the dark days Melissa had been in and out of psychiatric care as well as foster supervision until she was sixteen. The hospital treatment made Bob very angry. He was angry at the drugs and the 'therapy'. He was also angry at his mother for letting her be put into care. Melissa could hold a normal conversation and gave no impression of being weird or disturbed in any way. But that was what was wrong. Her spirit was gone. She never laughed, she never cried, she never enjoyed herself, she was never naughty. She was not the sister Bob remembered. She had difficulty holding down a job and never made any long term friends. She lived mostly on the dole and Bob couldn't help her much financially. Bob had enough trouble himself holding down a job and could only just meet the mortgage, credit card and loan payments on his truck. But in his case his antipathy to working was for different reasons. Bob was very hard working, very conscientious and would always see things through. He just couldn't abide authority, bureaucracy or working for people he didn't like. He asked Melissa if she wanted to trace their Dad. There was a simple, but final, 'No'. It was pretty much the same answer that she would give if you asked her to talk about any serious question: about emotions, money or life. Ask her about soap characters and she would suddenly become animated about their motivations, experiences and attitudes but ask her how she felt personally and the most detail you could expect was an inarticulate 'hmph' for bad or 'okay' for good.

It was a low spring tide and it abruptly turned and started to come back in. The first thing Bob noticed was a change in the wind direction. It was coming from the sea now. Much colder and more bracing than before. Still pleasant and refreshing but in a startling way that rushes forcefully into your open mouth and makes you gulp the air, or encourages you to turn your back to breathe facing the land. Bob let the rolling edge of the surf splash playfully over his boots but when a surge went over the top and down one sock he took the hint and tiptoed his way back from boulder to boulder, around the side of the beach that had not yet been overrun with water, and reluctantly made his way back up the hill. He resolved that he would try and trace his father when this job was over. He wasn't expecting a magical 'kiss and make up' family reunion but he was expecting to be able to ask the questions of his father that he'd always wanted to ask his mother. Why did things fall apart? Why did he not stay in touch? Was there another woman? Was it Melissa?

8. Going Underground

Back in the garden things were progressing ever more slowly. Guy was exhausted. He had been trying to dig down to get sufficient depth for the pond feature. The ground was poor, compacted and full of brick and stone detritus that would bring Guy's spade up in a juddering quiver every time he struck something. The lactic acid in his arms from the exertion was beginning to make them weak and jelly-like. Maya had noticed him begin to struggle and take longer and longer breathers in between digging. She came over and tried to help but the hole wasn't really big enough for two people to work in simultaneously. Reluctantly Guy let Maya take over for a while but she made as little headway as Guy. Maya blamed the spade which was a fairly cheap one and apt to bend rather than cut. Guy went to rummage around in Bob's truck and returned with the solution. A pickaxe. The only problem was lifting and swinging it.

By the time Guy had got the pickaxe above his head he could do little but let it drop under its own weight onto the bottom of the trench. It was a heavy duty tool, homemade by the look of it. Maya signalled for Guy to stop his second swing by raising her palm in front of his puffing red face like someone halting the traffic. With a frankly annoyed look on Guy's face he managed to stop.

'Let me lever up some of these,' she said, indicating the rubble with a trowel, 'you can then lift them, or break the larger pieces over the back of an iron bar that I can put underneath'. It was more sensible to dig them out one by one or break selected pieces than it was to swing the pickaxe or spade at random not knowing whether you were going to sink into soil or hit stone. 'A little more brains and less brawn I think, Guy'.

Guy said nothing. He knew Maya was right and he was annoyed with himself for getting so exhausted without much to show for it. He knew Bob would have finished this task hours ago by choosing the right tool and the right technique from the start.

Maya cleaned off the surface obstructions and probed around to find the softest places to dig. She marked the harder areas by paint spraying little crosses onto the soil. She then turned to Guy and said, 'Okay dig between the marks and then put the pickaxe on the edges and then hopefully we can lever up and shatter the bits of concrete, brick and stone.'

With the combined effect of rest, better technique and a little bit of adrenalin from annoyance at being told how to do the job, Guy really got into the swing of it. Maya scurried around the sides of the hole lifting stones and rubble like a wagtail dipping and bobbing around a rushing stream of water deftly grabbing flies before any danger of being engulfed by the unstoppable brook.

Maya noticed that they were getting quite a deep hole when, despite laying flat with her stomach over the side of the trench, her short arms could no longer reach anything at all. But Guy laboured on in a mindless trance of work. He felt the earth was getting easier and easier to penetrate with the heavy pickaxe. He even thought he could hear the soil trickling away below him when suddenly a tiny, tiny hand came up and grabbed the point of his pickaxe. Guy gasped. Wide eyed in astonishment he looked around for Maya to confirm that what he had seen had actually happened. But Maya had given up when she could no longer reach the stones and had gone back to her own work at the other end of the garden. Suddenly there was a scream from the other direction. Guy's body jerked like a body dangling from the hangman's noose, not knowing whether to look in the direction of the scream or keep his eyes on the tiny hand for fear he had only imagined it and that it would magically dissolve. His choice was made as the pale clean fingers unclasped the pickaxe point and slipped back into the earth. Guy turned to see Marjorie clasping her hand to her breast and gasping for air. Guy finally kicked his conscious self back into action and he leaped out of the hole in a single bound and was by Marjorie's side gently supporting her elbow. Her face was white and shaking as Maya came up and supported her other elbow. After Guy's redundant question, 'Are you all right?' nobody spoke. After working through a range of facial expressions and opening his mouth to speak but not being able to form a question Guy decided the best thing was to move Marjorie in the direction of her lounge. She was gently guided back into the house and laid down on the sofa. Her breathing recovered and she stopped shaking but she continued to stare wild-eyed at a blank point between the carpet and the skirting board.

'Should we call for an ambulance?' Maya asked.

'Give her a moment. I'm not sure there's anything more the matter with her than with me.'

'What do you mean?'

Guy was silent. It was if he didn't want to appear foolish by suggesting that there were pixies or fairies at the bottom of the garden and he wasn't a superstitious person. He knew that no matter how extraordinary it seemed there must be a perfectly rational explanation for what he had seen and suspected Marjorie had also seen. But he had no everyday words that he felt could adequately describe it. To him it was like a child-like dwarf's corpse from some horrible fusion of Carrie, Don't Look Now or a Hammer horror movie that had thrust its pale sinister fingers up out of the grave to grab him by the ankles and, no matter whether or not he shut his eyes, he couldn't rid himself of the additional image of Christopher Lee's blood gorged eyes bearing down on him through a mist shrouded graveyard.

Guy wanted to focus the imagery running through his brain on something more healthy and ordinary so he started to look around the room at the family photographs in the little alcoves by the fireplace and in a glass fronted cabinet between brandy glasses. The first thing he noticed was what was not there. There were no photographs of children or grandchildren. Not even brothers or sisters' or cousins' children. They were mostly signed photographs of Johnny in various ludicrous costumes – particularly Naval uniforms (always at a rank above ordinary seaman). There were very few of Marjorie, two in fact. One was fairly recent at some Village Hall do. It looked like a professional photographer's work. Everyone was sitting at a table at lunch, raising their glasses. Everyone was smiling and facing the camera. There was no food and when you looked closely no wine or water in the glasses. Perhaps it was a local newspaper photographer who had arrived to cover the event before the food was served. The second was black and white, and in a small frame. It was heavily creased, diagonally across the photograph, as if it had been kept in someone's pocket. It showed Marjorie as a stunningly attractive young woman with a friend or sister of about the same age. They were laughing and holding hands.

'Who is this in the photograph?' asked Guy, pointing at the small silver frame.

'Believe it or not that's me. Time has been a little unkind.'

'Yes I know. I mean I knew it was you. I don't think time has been too unkind to you. I wondered who the other person was.'

'Ah.'

There was a long, long pause as Marjorie stared back out into the garden where so recently Guy had been grappling with an unexpected visitor from the underworld.

'That's Becky. She was my friend at college. Arts and Drama college. I had dreams of being an actress. So did she. We were in a chorus line in a musical when she was 'spotted'. There weren't many great Shakespearean roles for women (still aren't) or any decent character work in those days. It was kick your legs high and show your knickers and just hope for a sugar daddy to fall in love with you. Well she certainly found one. She married Johnny.'

'Are you saying she was Johnny's first wife, before you?'

'Yes.'

'Presumably you all fell out at some point.'

'Oh no, not really. She still writes to me although I've not seen her for years. I speak to her on the telephone sometimes when

Johnny's not around. Needless to say Johnny can't stand her. He doesn't like me having that photograph on display. He says it "sets his bile off" so that's why I put it there. That, and to remind myself I could always do the same and find a life outside of Johnny.'

'What happened to end Johnny's first marriage then?' asked Maya. Guy shot her a cross look as if to say it was none of her business and she shouldn't have asked.

'I was jealous at first, and puzzled. I'd always had the boyfriends and she tended to pick up my rejects. Well she paid me back royally for that one in the end. Becky enjoyed life as a minor celebrity for a while. Johnny was starting to get recognised in the West End and there was talk of a lucrative Hollywood deal. I think it was when that didn't materialise that she first started to have doubts. Johnny's always been one to build his hopes on sand and I guess he must have spun her many phoney lines; I remember he promised her a dinner with Cary Grant which never happened. Ironically it was the Second World War that put paid to Johnny's ambitions. He desperately wanted to get into War pictures but all the best parts were given to people who were already established and Johnny refused to do the little cameos that might have got him noticed. It was the ideal time when so many good actors were called up and otherwise occupied. But Johnny wanted the big part – the hero role that would catapult him to fame. He wanted to do American movies about the British Navy but the Americans were never interested in glorifying the British or other Allied war efforts – even after the war. There were collaborative army based films but the Navy and Air Force ones tended to be all British (or European émigrés). Besides he was too young. By the time he had learnt his craft, and had a few good roles under his belt, everyone wanted to forget the war and make kitchen sink dramas.'

Maya asked, 'But what about you? What about your career?'

'Sorry. I've lived my life through Johnny for so long it becomes a habit just to talk about him. After all, it's all *he* ever wants to talk about. As I said there were not many good parts around. I'm a tone deaf singer and dance like a donkey on roller skates. So what I really wanted were some dramatic character roles. Apparently female character actresses had to be older and uglier. The parts I got offered were either singing and dancing or had practically no dialogue. You were just expected to shriek a lot, swoon and get kissed. I put up with the chorus line for Becky's sake but when she left to become a celebrity party goer with Johnny I decided to chuck it in. I was on the point of getting rid of my Equity card when it occurred to me I had always been good at art and could find a way of combining the two and stay in the theatre. I went back stage, just painting flats at first, then into full scale set design.'

'Flats?'

'Not people's apartments. They're the big boards in the background that you move around to make differently shaped spaces. Then I started messing around with the Proscenium Arch – you know between the audience and the play. I tried to bring it forward and lower the edge of the stage so that the front few rows were in amongst the action. All sorts of stuff. If you promise not to yawn I'll show you some of my scrapbooks and models.'

Her earlier shock and paleness seemed to have evaporated as Marjorie led Guy and Maya into a spare bedroom. It had been converted into a glorified office and had piles of scrapbooks and memorabilia in carefully labelled cardboard boxes. They were a little dusty and Maya sneezed as Marjorie brought the first of the boxes out. In it was a beautiful scale model of a Theatre complete with rows of seats, different curtains and dolls house furniture on the stage. Marjorie showed Guy and Maya how the different scenes in the play were achieved through subtle changes, how the action went into and around the audience, how the lighting and sound effects contributed to the set design. After the third box Guy was praising her work enthusiastically and asking her whether she was still working. She had retired but had been actively working long after Johnny's acting, not to mention any supermarket openings, prize award giving and after dinner speeches, had well and truly dried up. In fact it was Marjorie and not Johnny that had bought this house, that had a reasonable pension from money put by and that was funding the garden makeover. For a while she had been the most sought after designer in the West End Theatre circuit and had a highly lucrative consultancy service she offered to a number of leading European and American stage designers.

Guy and Maya were amazed. It wasn't just the quality of the work. It was the discomforting thought that, behind the quiet exteriors of many a retired couple, there were people who had led full and interesting lives like Marjorie. It was the thought that all of us were so much the poorer for not bothering to ask 'older people' about the entirety of their lives, loves, hopes, dreams and experiences. It was the unthinking and casual assumption that pensioners were somehow born pensioners; that it was a profession they aspired to, and that their only occupation was the minor irritations of shopping, TV murder mysteries or twitching the curtain to find out what the neighbours were up to. Guy felt it was such a shame that this secret remained locked away in dusty cardboards in a room where the light bulb had long since blown and nobody had bothered to replace it. There was a photograph of one design in particular that struck him. It was a scene for a play called 'The Picnic' and was loosely based around a painting he knew by the French Impressionist

Édouard Manet. It was an ordinary square stage in which a naked woman and a group of fully clothed actors sat together deep in conversation but it was the backdrop to the scene that intrigued Guy. It had some interesting trompe l'oeil effects with foliage clipped so that it was much smaller towards the centre and thereby increasing the sense of depth. It made quite a small area seem like a large park simply by tricking the eye with a false perspective. In the centre an arch was created by two sapling trees bent over and tied at the apex. The saplings were only about ten feet tall but seemed much taller because everyone was sat on the ground, not standing, and they had been planted on raised mounds.

It was just the sort of finishing touch that would help Guy personalise the eating area in the garden and, in his excitement to get on with making the alteration, Guy asked if it would be alright if he could be excused. In his single-mindedness he had even forgotten the incident with the hand. Marjorie was more than happy not to talk about that though she must have felt that Guy was just bored, and rude. That's what Maya thought anyway and stayed talking longer than she would have done otherwise to compensate. She didn't regret it. She didn't recognise any of the plays Marjorie mentioned. Guy was the sort who had read the arts pages of national newspapers at the time and would have known them, at least in review. Nonetheless Maya was still enchanted by the whole magical world of make-believe and stagecraft. It reminded her of all the dressing up and street processions she had witnessed as a child where her normally grumpy, humdrum or sad neighbours were suddenly transformed by makeup and costumes into mythical beasts from fantastic tales and legends.

Afterwards, as she made her way back up to the Bed and Breakfast later than intended, Maya wondered how Marjorie could bear to live at the other end of England to the London she knew and loved, how she could bear to not still be a part of it all, and why? Was she happy? What was retirement all about? Was it any good? Her parents never 'retired', they wouldn't have dreamed of it. They just went on working as long as health and mobility would permit. That was what life was all about. Whether it made them happier she couldn't say but she couldn't help thinking that something was missing from Marjorie's current lifestyle, and it wasn't just having a nice garden.

9. The brightest angel falls furthest

Guy and Maya came to work next morning in Bob's truck. They were seen coming into the garden by Marjorie. Guy opened his mouth to speak and ask her if they had really seen what he thought he saw but Marjorie abruptly turned her back and disappeared to busy herself in the kitchen. Neither of them had mentioned what they had seen in the garden on the previous day to anyone yet. Guy hadn't even said anything to Maya. Maya was curious about it but didn't want Guy to know how curious by pestering him. 'If either of them want to tell me what it was all about then they'll tell me', she thought.

Guy inspected the site and gathered his thoughts to organise the tasks for the day ahead. Number one – make good the hole at the bottom of the trench for the pond. He casually glanced into the trench that had been so difficult to excavate. There was no hole. In fact it looked as though the bottom had been nicely smoothed with some fine graded soil. There had been a bit of rain overnight and Guy just shrugged and put it down to the settling effect that any water would have had on the soil levels. It may even have gummed up the small hole where the pickaxe had penetrated into nothingness. Number two – line it with fine sand. Number three – put in, cut and shape the butyl liner.

Although the trench was largely formal in shape there were a few irregular semi-circular shapes on either side which were meant to represent the fins of basking sharks seen off the coast of Cornwall each summer. The trench was fourteen foot long – about the size of an average shark. These beautiful and harmless creatures were mentioned by Johnny when they had originally come down to accept the brief. This had given Guy the idea. Bob was going to line the pond in concrete. Guy could mix the concrete but wasn't sufficiently confident about cutting the wood to batten the shaping of the concrete against the pond wall. He also thought it might crack and so took the easier option of purchasing a liner. He would mask the edging with a combination of soil, stone and shallow planting. Maya would be able to improvise with a few carpet forming bog plants.

In fact Maya had her own ideas of what to do next and was already busy at work setting about the bamboo screen and grasses. Her approach was very different from Guy's. Guy was a great procrastinator. When he worked then he would work quickly but to Maya he seemed to spend an inordinate amount of time just looking at the garden, thinking and planning before lifting a trowel. She preferred to get on with it and, if necessary, change or tweak the design several times as it went along.

The morning wore on. Bob popped by and harrumphed about the shoddy change of materials. There was no sign of Marjorie. She normally popped out at about eleven with some tea, coffee and delicious home-baked biscuits. Guy and Maya slaked their thirst from the outside tap and got on with it. With Maya's efforts to start the first of the planting the overall design was beginning to look softer, more intriguing and more mature. Both of them worked through without thinking of stopping for lunch.

Later on a police car called at the house and Marjorie ushered what, to Guy, looked like a teenage policeman into the lounge.

'Someone must have found Johnny and they're asking if she wants to take him back!' joked Maya. Whatever it was, the policeman left after a few minutes to sit in his car and radio through back to the Station. After a few minutes of checking his notes, and speaking, he left. As soon as the car drew away Marjorie's curtain fluttered, the door opened and she sped off down in the direction of the harbour. She was wearing a large brown headscarf which seemed to cover half her face. It wasn't particularly windy or cold.

The time was now about 3pm and Johnny rolled up obviously expecting his wife to be at home. You could tell that because when he turned the door handle and it didn't yield (being locked) he still attempted to walk through the door – getting a bit of a nose bashing as a result. With some cursing and fumbling about in his capacious tweeds he found his key and entered.

'Well it's not Johnny then, whatever it is', said Maya. 'Can we get something to eat?'

'Yeah sure, but I don't want to stop. Can you fetch a pasty?'

'Fine. What sort?'

'Something veggie or Cheese and Bacon would be fine. Do you need some cash? There's some in my jacket', said Guy pointing to a crumpled coat hanging over a garden fork that had been impaled in a pile of earth.

'Okay'.

Maya washed the dirt off her hands using the cold water from the outside tap, shook her hands vigorously and rubbed them against her jean thighs and walked over to liberate the cash from Guy's coat. Walking down to the pasty shop opposite the Golden Lion she paused to take a view of activity in the harbour over the wall. The tide was out and the fishing boats were all lurching at crazy angles on the hard sand chained securely as if they might otherwise glide away like ships of the desert. A pair of Labradors were romping about on the edge of the sea trying to rescue a well chewed tennis ball repeatedly thrown out by their owner. A small girl in a bright blue bikini was squatting on the edge of some rocks with a net on a 6 foot bamboo stick which she was finding too large to turn around in the confined space under the cliffs. An old couple were playing a rather stiff, and slow, game of beach football with their grandson who insisted on running around in mad circles like a dog chasing its tail. Maya took a deep breath of the fresh sea air. It felt good. She had never really understood the English predilection for the seaside holiday. It seemed so quaint, so like double-decker buses and red coated soldiers with huge black busbies outside Buckingham Palace. In an age of global travel to hot and exotic destinations, and the exciting prospect of space tourism, she wasn't sure it was still relevant or would still survive. But it did. And she was glad.

A Cornwall Council van pulled up beside her and a couple of gruesome-looking heavies jumped out of the back door. From the driver's seat a middle aged and very respectable looking lady got out. She had a jagged white streak of hair down the middle of her carefully set grey hair and wore sharply pointed black-framed glasses. "No. 34", she said. Behind them the same police car she had seen earlier drew quietly up behind. The young policeman didn't get out, just sat there and watched.

The lady knocked on the door of Number 34, waving and shooshing away the two heavies to wait slightly to one side out of direct sight of the door. The door opened and the lady stepped in without waiting to be invited. Seconds later she emerged clasping a small boy by the wrist. The mother, who had opened the door, appeared distraught and slightly dazed. She clearly didn't understand what was going on, or at least why. When she moved to speak to her son one of the heavies stepped in her path and kept moving around in front of her to block her path without actually touching her.

Shoppers, idly passing by, started to stop and look but the mother was now silent. She knew it was pointless to persist although, by now, the boy himself was starting to cry as he was bundled roughly into the van. The lady got in as if to console him but the boy was now pulling away and looking accusingly at his bruised wrist. She turned away, switched on the engine and started to drive off even before the heavies had closed the doors after hurriedly getting back in. The policeman looked bored and began to shuffle some paperwork. The mother just stared forwards, not seeing anyone and not hearing any enquiry as to whether she was alright. Finally she just turned around and went back indoors slamming the door. The policeman drove off.

Maya turned to stare out across the harbour. She was essentially a very private person who hated to interfere or speculate about other people's lives but she had been troubled by the look on the mother's face. She recognised that feeling of helplessness, in a world where everyone appeared to be bigger and more powerful than her, where, at any moment, the certainties and safety of her life could be trampled on in complete disregard by strangers. She felt alone, and, in feeling alone, felt at one with the mother. But there must be a husband, mustn't there? I suppose not necessarily.

Maya was now looking across the harbour to the hillside cottages on the other side. She noticed a pair of roofers replacing a section of tiles. One of them was rather gingerly and carefully crossing the ridge to hand a mobile phone to the other. The person taking the phone handed it back after only a few seconds and slid down a ladder braced against some scaffolding. There was something about the reckless haste of his descent that answered Maya's question about a husband. Sure enough within 60 seconds the man was in the street outside Number 34. But instead of flying through the front door he hesitated, looked at Maya, then ran off further up the street. Perhaps it was just a coincidence.

Meanwhile the mother had appeared at the front door and looked down the street. The other roofer slowly ambled up and stopped to speak to her, 'I thought he was with you,' he said in answer to her question. 'Oh no,' she sobbed, 'oh no… he's gone to him, that's what he's gone and done, he's gone to him. You've got to stop him – for God's sake.'

'Why? He's got a perfect right to see his own child.'

'No, not him, I don't mean HIM.'

'Then who, for God's sake?'

'Social Services think it's my Peter but it's not. I know exactly who it is and so do half the mothers round here. You men don't see anything unless it's something right under your noses. Something you can eat… or drink… or have sex with.' At this statement she broke down in sobs and the roofer turned her gently around by the shoulders and led her indoors.

Maya remembered she was hungry and hurried down to the Pasty shop to see if it was closed. It wasn't and she put all other thoughts out of her head and hurried back up to Guy with the hot pasties taking a little extra for herself which she secretly devoured on the way back up to the garden.

Lunch was ravaged in rapid appreciative grunts without any conversation. Both Guy and Maya then lay back on the new turf to rest contentedly and watch the clouds gently drifting in the sea breezes.

'Tell me about your wife Guy.' she asked.

'What's there to tell? Julie means nothing to me any more. She's just an item on the monthly accounts, like the gas or the electric only more expensive.'

'Did you have children?'

'No. I guess that might have made a difference. Who knows?'

'You didn't want them?'

'We couldn't.'

There was a long pause. The day was fairly quiet with only the distant sound of gulls crying and what sounded like a Police or Fire Engine siren getting slightly nearer. Guy was tempted to call it a day. He started to review the tasks and whether it was worth starting any new work. Maya was lost in her own thoughts about family and relationships; about her father and the long periods of time he would stay working apart from her mother in other countries. The siren got closer. She could now hear sounds of people shouting and glass breaking.

'I think we need to go,' she said.

'Why?'

'Well, it's just that…I want to see what happens.' With that she was off. Guy was puzzled. Slowly he got up and followed her down into the top of Fore Street. The noise of shouting became louder. A crowd of people of both sexes and all ages were gathered in the street. A bay window had been shattered and a group of youths were throwing stones, sticks, flower pots, grocery and eggs at the house. The front door was broken and hanging off its hinges. There were desperate but muffled shouts coming from inside. Maya recognised the two roofers she had seen earlier – they were dragging a limp body out of the house although one of them seemed to be half helping and half remonstrating with the other one. As they emerged a great cheer went up from the crowd who now converged on the unfortunate victim. There was kicking, punching, spitting and who knows what else going on in the centre. From behind Guy two policemen pushed their way through knocking Guy temporarily off balance into Maya's arms. The policemen made their way into the rest of the crowd which seemed to mysteriously part like the waves in front of Moses. Some of the stragglers on the outer edges started to melt away as well but others in the centre started chanting something that Guy and Maya couldn't make out. The policemen finally emerged from the centre of the crowd dragging the offender under the arms. To Maya's astonishment it wasn't either of the roofers but the vicar they were taking away. He was filthy, bruised and bloodied with his scant white hair no longer in a "comb-over" – more of a "comb-spiral".

A few were continuing to kick and abuse the poor vicar. By this time Bob had also turned up, attracted by the noise, and asked, 'Are they chapel? Don't they like C of E?' Guy couldn't believe what he was seeing and simply couldn't answer Bob's jokey question. He was too outraged. He pulled one youth aside that was taking a swing with his leg only to be confronted by Marjorie who caught the vicar an almighty smack in the jaw with a heavily laden handbag. This caused the policemen to drop him on the pavement. The vicar sprang up and ran away. He disappeared down an alley leading past the church with the policemen and the crowd in hot pursuit. As the alley was only wide enough for one person at a time there was a lot of jostling for position and this seemed to give the vicar a head start. 'Is it a local custom,' asked Bob, 'like the Furry Dance? Can we all join in?'

'I think it has to do with the choir boys,' Maya said. 'The one who attacked the vicar first; he's the father of a boy that I saw in the church the other day. I think it was the same boy that was taken in for interview, or maybe taken into care, earlier this afternoon. I thought, at the time, he had the look of a boy who knew too much. It was as if he had been forced to grow up too quickly and had been given a terrible secret that it wasn't fair to give him at that age.'

Guy didn't really understand the full implications of what Maya was presuming but got enough of a flavour of it for him to lose all sympathy for the vicar. The three of them decided to make their way back to the garden to make sure that none of their tools were taken in the melee.

Too late.

As they rounded the corner the vicar was being led out from Johnny and Marjorie's garden by the policeman. None of the tools had gone but enough people had kept up with the police pursuit to trample the whole site and rip the butyl liner. The vicar now had the policeman's coat over his head and was being bundled into the squad car. Guy noticed something fall out of the vicar's right hand as he got in.

When the car drove off he looked in the gutter at the side of the road. It was part of a squashed, and broken, carrot.

10. Animal Magic

When Guy and Maya assessed the damage it was not as bad as they had feared. Bizarrely some plant ties and a couple of plant labels had gone but no tools and no plants. The liner would have to be replaced but fortunately Guy had ordered a large roll and had enough left to place it directly over the torn one. He also attempted a patch seal on the original to provide a double lining. There was a small amount of aeration, raking and reshaping of soil levels where these had been scuffed and compressed by the trampling hordes but, all in all, it could have been a lot worse.

They were still a little behind schedule though and Guy's main concern was an overrun on labour which could make the whole project uneconomical. He was only paying Bob a nominal retainer for non-working days based on him giving advice and doing some of the phoning and paperwork but it was taking Guy and Maya a lot longer to carry out the tasks than it would have done with the three of them. Guy would have to waive any wages for himself and they were certainly overrunning on expenses (which Bob was still getting). Bob had some sort of self-employed insurance scheme which he was also claiming on but wasn't very forthcoming to Guy about the details.

Meanwhile, he argued, if he was needed for advice he had to stay locally.

Bob took his new role of "supervisor" very seriously and was quick to point out any inadequacies in Guy and Maya's work. Today Johnny seemed to have linked up with his new best buddy Bob and was also offering horticultural and building hints and tips.

Maya was sawing down some thick bamboo canes into irregular lengths and using them to drag an old twisted rope across to make a dwarf barrier in front of the planted bamboo. She left gaps for interplanting but Johnny kept telling her she had slanted the saw cuts away from perpendicular or got the length wrong (which was deliberate) and should measure them properly.

Guy was trying to level and sow a small lawn area. Bob had a long spirit level which he kept walking along behind Guy and tutting and drawing breath through his teeth without actually saying anything. In Bob's world flat was always dead flat. He was a geometrical obsessive. Guy was working on the principle that although he wanted a flat area to contrast with the surrounding slopes and banks he also wanted it to look flat in relation to the house. The damp proof course on the house which was painted bituminous black below the pink rose walls had a slight slope. Perhaps it wasn't always that way but had settled, like many properties in the area, on top of shifting mine workings. In order for the lawn to look flat in relation to the house Guy was convinced he needed to put a slight slope in and judge it by eye.

Work progressed slowly through the morning. Suddenly Johnny looked up into the sky as if scanning the horizon for dive bombing seagulls and then sped off into the house. A few minutes later he emerged clasping two Sundae glasses filled to the brim with some noxious pink liquid. He took an enormous draft from one and passed the other to Bob. Bob lifted one eyebrow. Johnny volunteered the answer – 'It's called Pink Links after a recipe I picked up at St. Enodoc Golf Club.'

'Wow', gasped Bob, 'that'll ruin your handicap.' Guy exchanged a world-weary look with Maya. No refreshments for the troops. Again.

Maya went over to the outdoor tap and filled a small plastic cup. She needn't have bothered. The gesture was lost on Johnny who had already disappeared into the kitchen to try a new mind-bending variation on the 'Pink Links' called the 'Stinky Pink Winkle'. Bob countered with the Crème de Menthe based 'Pond Slime' and the sludge brown 'Zombie Woof'.

Guy finally lost his temper, and he was a man always slow to lose his temper, when Johnny fell into the empty dry pond with the eye bogglingly psychedelic 'Enola Gay's Fat Greek Wedding Surprise'.

'Sorry old chap – was trying to break the glass or was it the plate?'

'If you break that lining I'll…' but the sentence tailed off into silent exasperation as Guy realised he couldn't afford to give Johnny the ear-bashing he so richly deserved. Not until he's paid. In any case it was his pond and if he wanted to jump in it and ruin it that was down to him.

Bob – who could sense Guy's incandescence more easily than the thick-skinned Johnny – suggested they go for a little fresh air to clear the palate before their next round.

Guy and Maya waited until their 'supervisors' were out of sight then downed tools for a well-earned rest and a bite to eat.

Johnny and Bob walked off arm in arm singing some kind of improvised sea shanty based loosely on the phrase "Home, home from the Sea" but which had become "Moan, moan from the settee" as Johnny berated his better half and their domestic bliss.

Our crooners successfully negotiated the Golden Lion (topping up on HSD) and the bar of the Slipway Hotel (with a Doom Bar) from which they were finally expelled after Johnny got into a dispute with the barmaid about slipping her a couple of Inch's. He had meant to order 'Two pints of Inch's Stonehouse Cider please' but it got lost in a welter of innuendo about the size of his manhood and when he undid his flies to prove a point he was politely shown the door by the barmaid, shift manager and one of the more portly cooks for backup.

The two disgraced troubadours took a wrong turning from the nearby public toilets and found themselves walking up the lane to the coastal path. It was slow progress, stopping for frequent breathers and to stop the walls and railings from wobbling by leaning on them to steady them. Nonetheless they were eventually up onto the headland with the village sprawled picturesquely at the foot of the valley leading down to the sea. In front of them they could see north up the coast to Tintagel and (on a particularly clear day) the small island of Lundy on the hazy horizon. To the south was Lobber Point. Bob had the dangerous notion to go for a swim and started to scramble and tumble down the path to the nearest access point. Johnny followed slightly reluctantly behind. Once onto the shore Bob stripped down to his white cotton boxers and started gingerly dancing over the stony beach. Beach was probably the wrong word for it at Lobber Point: there was no sand, just big stones and small stones. Before Bob could get as far as the sea he decided the soft white soles of his sensitive feet had suffered enough and sat down with a splash into the nearest large tidal pool. Even at the height of summer this was barely tepid but Bob seemed to be very content so Johnny cast off his shoes, rolled up his trouser legs and sat on the edge of a rock by the pool.

For the first time since they had left the garden they became silent, almost contemplative. A long time seemed to pass although it was probably only about 10 minutes.

Johnny noticed that a snorting Walrus sound accompanied the regular rhythm of the waves beating against the rocks. It was Bob. His head was slumped forward on his chest and he was fast asleep and snoring soundly to the soothing rhythm of the breaking waves.

Johnny started to half doze as well. The combined hypnotic effect of synchronised snoring and the sun's warmth dragged heavily on his own eyelids until with an almighty snort and exhalation of air Bob suddenly woke himself up. 'Christ, look at the tide!' he shouted.

It was true. The tide had sneaked around them and almost cut them off from returning up the beach. One of Bob's socks was already Atlantic bound and they needed to paddle onto higher rocks and then jump back to the foot of a slippery rock face which they now had to scramble up to leave the beach. This was no mean feat, with one of Bob's wrist out of action and the other carrying his remaining clothes and with Johnny's legs still having limited functionality. At the top they collapsed into a single exhausted heap on a grassy knoll.

'Was I snoring?' asked Bob, 'I think that's what woke me up or a seagull.'

'My dear boy that wasn't a seagull, you were sending them home like a Rhino in heat.'

Johnny then sat up and proceeded to demonstrate what was either intended to be a parody of Bob's snoring or a female Rhino's orgasm or both. Certainly both interpretations were credible.

Johnny then proceeded to run through what seemed to be the rest of Noah's ark, both large and small animals in turn, with running commentary on various species' mating behaviour and accompanying sounds. It was a hilarious tour de force and even Bob, who could do MacDonald's Farm with the best of them, was in tears of laughter.

'They should have had you instead of that Johnny Morris geezer on Animal Magic or whatever kid's nature programmes they have these days. Some of those sounds are even quite authentic and I'm pretty hot on my nature documentaries.'

'I *have* done a few "growl-overs" as it happens. They don't do them now as everything has to be authentic. But in the early days they quite often found they had got some really good pictures with poor sound. They either had to patch over some unrelated recordings or get an imitator, sometimes a combination of both, just to get the timing absolutely right. Once your looks fade you have to go into sound. I've done more radio and advertising voiceovers than anything else in the last twenty years. There's some damn good radio if you look out for it. Well…listen out for it I mean.'

'Do you do requests? For example could you do a tiger mating with a Gnu?'

'I can do the Flanders and Swann song but you'd have to know your part. Or I can do a little drama for you with the greatest of pleasure.'

Johnny set the scene. The lonely confused tiger, nobody understood him. The other tigers didn't like him. His own mother had been tragically killed by a safari-suited handlebar-moustachioed hunter in the deepest darkest jungle. He was ripped from the dying mother tiger's teat by rough native bearers and brought up in Bombay zoo on Gnu's milk. He couldn't understand as a young teenage tiger his confused feelings when let loose in the Gnu enclosure. Whether to eat, or make love to, the lovely, pale, female Gnus. It felt so guilty and yet so good. 'What was a poor tiger to do?' he asked rhetorically, then Johnny started making the confused and startled noises of the Gnus, the ferocious and then tender low growls of the tiger. Then Johnny managed to do both sounds at once in a climactic crescendo of ecstasy. In fact it sounded like several animals calling simultaneously. Johnny gave up and started coughing, although it sounded as if the tiger's growl still echoed around the rocks in the bay as if in response and challenge to Johnny's mating call.

11. Fearful Symmetry

Johnny decided he was getting cold and his throat felt sore. He knew just the right cure for his dehydration. More alcohol. So the two of them set off back to Johnny's house. It was starting to get dark by the time they returned to an anxious Marjorie. Bob didn't want to continue drinking, with or without the withering collective glare of Marjorie, Guy and Maya bearing down on him, so he said his goodbyes to Johnny on the doorstep. He praised Johnny's mimicry again but Johnny wouldn't take the compliment. 'That tiger wasn't all me you know,' he said rather cryptically, in a low tone. The problem with Johnny's stage whispers was that you could normally hear them within a half-mile radius and this was certainly within Maya's hearing and probably Guy's.

Guy had a word with Bob before they left for their digs. He asked if Bob could do some light work tomorrow. The implication was clear. He wasn't here for a holiday. Keeping the client happy was one thing but Guy felt that Bob was not taking a fully professional approach. Bob got a bit huffy and grumpy but he knew Guy was right. He turned to Maya who was half way through planting a small forest of baby purple Cordylines.

'I'll give you a hand with that tomorrow – just the one. Hand that is.'

True to his word Bob was first on site in the morning and had planted a good deal of the remaining Cordylines by the time Maya had arrived. They weren't exactly in the places Maya had intended but she didn't say anything as she was grateful for the help.

Maya set Bob a few other tasks that could be more or less achieved by a mono-limbed gardener and settled down to the more satisfying task of finishing the pond, trying the marginals in different positions and looking at them from all 360 angles until she was entirely satisfied. 'I need a few pebbles. Do you mind if I go down to the beach Guy?'

Now that there were three of them (or two and a half pairs of arms) actively working on the project things seemed to be going a lot faster and Guy was feeling less mean about time. 'No, in fact you've been working very hard the last couple of days. Why don't you take an early lunch and pick up some pebbles on your way back. I've got to go over to Tintagel this afternoon for something anyway. Thinking about it I'm not sure this area is great for the sort of beautifully rounded pebbles you get on my beloved Chesil Beach but better use something local anyway, in character with the granite and slate or you could imitate those beautiful zig-zag folds of green and red Serpentine rocks. You're welcome to come and try Tintagel if you want. I don't know what the beach is like there. There's not much of it at the foot of the castle although I read in the local rag about some rockfall or landslip in Merlin's Cave. You could try there.'

This was an invitation that Maya had been waiting for; so she accepted the offer of a lift but not to collect rocks and pebbles. She hurried to the nearest shop to get whatever would be the quickest snack lunch (which turned out to be a sausage roll that might have been fresh once and a nearly ripe banana) and then got back to site. It seemed an age ago now that she had told a disinterested Guy about St. Endellienta and the fact that she wanted to see if there was any other information she could find about the female saint who loved animals and earned the respect of the local farmers. She had asked in one of the gift shops that had a few local history booklets if they had anything about her but they had nothing. They had suggested the Tourist Information centre in Tintagel though. Maya had rushed back to the garden and caught Guy and persuaded him to take her there sometime but nothing had ever come of it and Guy had clearly forgotten. If push came to shove she could have driven herself but despite having the necessary license she wasn't keen to drive Bob's truck through these narrow lanes and the fact that Guy was going anyway seemed too good an opportunity to miss. The Information Centre, when she found it at the top of the village, had a fascinating collection of stories about Cornish saints and, tucked away in the middle of a general book about the early Saints in Cornwall, were a few tantalising fragments about St. Endellienta. Maya bought the book but didn't have time to look at properly as Guy had agreed to pick her up near Tintagel church (another place she wanted to see).

Maya was surprised the Church was a way outside the village on the clifftop away from the centre of the village so she took a side road - the aptly named Vicarage Hill – and enjoyed the walk up there to the isolated spot where St. Materiana overlooks Tintagel Castle. This was part of her reason for wanting to visit: to see the ruin associated with King Arthur but she was also intrigued to find out more about another female saint called Materiana or Madrun or Madryn. She arrived but couldn't get in so sat on the graveyard wall facing the sea and consulted her new book. Apparently Materiana was the eldest of three daughters of King Vortimer the Blessed and who ruled over Gwent in 5th century Wales with her husband Prince Ynyr. Although there is a church dedicated to her in Trawsfynydd in North Wales there are two in Cornwall: Tintagel and it's mother church the Minster, half a mile east of Boscastle in the Valency Valley where Meteriana is said to be buried. Although this made her seem a lot more real and tangible than Endeliienta there also seemed to be a suggestion that she represented Matrona the Roman pagan goddess of motherhood. From what Maya had already read about the saints she suspected that there was a real layer in which powerful women had built the society, beliefs and customs in the pagan and early Christian era only to become overlain with multiple personalities and stories of which she guessed guys with swords probably sold more books when medieval romances became the fashion.

Maya's musings were interrupted when she got a call on her recently borrowed mobile to say that Guy was tied up fetching some materials from a builder's merchant and would be another half hour. So Maya walked onto the nearest stretch of the coast path away from the monastic island associated with the King Arthur legend. Maya wasn't interested in going over the footbridge and climbing up to the ruined Castle for several reasons. Firstly the Knights of the Round Table suddenly seem to represent a very bloke-ish sort of mythical history that she wasn't entirely comfortable with. All that manly swashbuckling and sword wielding was the stuff of comic book superheroes as far as she was concerned with Lancelot being just as foolish and impetuous as the cuckolded Arthur. Secondly there were too many steps to go up and she was slightly scared of heights but would never admit it. Thirdly she instinctively felt she wanted to walk back in the direction of Port Isaac and in the direction of St. Endellion or Endellienta.

She soon came across an old mine working where the cliff had been whittled away to leave high chimney stacks of unusable material. These must have been taken direct out to sea as it seemed so difficult to drag them back up the steep slope overland. There were the ghostly brick shadows of former buildings long since abandoned. In some of the cracked and empty window frames tree seedlings and other plants were beginning to take hold. A young Peregrine falcon and his or her prey aerially danced amongst the crumbling shapes before the pigeon was cornered in a blind crevasse. Maya didn't see the kill but saw an explosion of grey and white feathers floating out to sea on the stiff swirling breezes.

She wanted to explore this forgotten industrial relic but the slope was too steep for her and she thought that time was getting on. When she returned to the church Guy was already waiting by the truck in the rough area of puddles and craters that passed for a car park. He hadn't been waiting long though – he had only just arrived – but he allowed Maya to feel guilty anyway.

'I'm afraid I still haven't got the pebbles. Shall I get them in Port Isaac?'

Guy looked at his watch and said maybe she could get them this evening. So Maya had to wait before being let off the leash again but the afternoon passed quickly enough. Bob was a great help to them both and she realised how much she missed his banter when working with Guy alone. Guy was easy to work with and very kind. But you never knew quite where you were with him because he left so many things unsaid.

With a cursory 'Right, that's it then', Guy packed up his more expensive tools, leaving the rest in Johnny and Marjorie's outhouse, and was back off to the B&B for a shower. Maya decided to head straight out to the coastal path where Bob and Johnny had been the previous day. Although she didn't know precisely where this was she thought she would head south from the Port and explore. When she reached the stream above the beach, she turned to follow it up the valley, and then through thin woodland up over the hill. There was an ancient but rather dilapidated Manor House brooding over the ploughed fields. Maya couldn't get close enough to determine whether it was now used as a farmhouse or was still owned by the landed gentry. Someone at the B&B had lent her some DVDs of the original TV series called 'Poldark' and she thought she recognised the house from one of the scenes. The eponymous hero of the series had fallen on hard times through some poor mining investments and was forced to contemplate engaging in (or at least turning a blind eye to) smuggling.

Maya headed over the adjacent fields and tried to find her way back to the coast. She followed a signpost indicating Port Quinn but didn't know that it had twisted in the wind and was actually pointing in the wrong direction. She passed some derelict stone farm buildings. She thought at first they were part of some mine working as there was a rusted wheel, cogs and winch until she realised it was just tackle for taking heavy loads (sacks presumably) up to a high doorway in a barn. From somewhere inside the barn she thought she could hear a small, pitiful, but very occasional, cry. She looked around for a doorway but the barn had solid walls on all four sides and no other means of access other than the hatch high in the side. She knew she should just walk away but she couldn't bear the thought that maybe a kitten had fallen in and couldn't get out. She looked around for a farmhouse or any possible owner of the buildings but the whole range of buildings just looked disused.

If she climbed on the rusting wheel, she thought, she would be able to shin up the chain to the hook above the hatch. She checked her pocket for the precious mobile phone that Guy and Bob had given her. It was there. It was switched on. Unknown to her the battery was also a gnat's whisker from being totally flat. Guy and Bob had forgotten to explain the niceties of charging the battery – in fact they hadn't even given her the charger.

With her light weight and strong wiry frame she made short work of climbing the chain and although the hook swivelled ominously in its wooden housing it was fairly secure. Maya had given it a good yank to make sure before she started up it. She had to set up a swinging motion backwards and forwards on the hook, gradually increasing the ark of the swing, until she could get her trainers to grip on the ledge of the hatch and pull herself over to the side of the frame. Whatever was in the barn she couldn't see because after the bright sunlight everything inside was dark. But she could hear more clearly now a shuffling sound as if small padded feet were stepping on thin straw covering a concrete floor.

She dropped onto the floor herself by swinging agilely over a crossed wooden beam. There was a more rapid frightened scurrying of feet and then a renewed crying. It was a meow – a rough, throaty, but clearly infant, meow. Maya's eyes began to adjust and she tentatively stepped forward pushing her feet along through the straw without lifting them hardly at all. She didn't want to step on anything by mistake. The shuffling sound her feet made sounded like that she had heard earlier and then there it was – a huge orangey stripy kitten.

'Ahhhh', she involuntarily spoke, 'don't be afraid. I've come to rescue you.'

Her own voice was the last sound she heard.

12. No Show Flower Show

That time of year had arrived again. The Port Isaac Horticultural Society Annual Show. Not a major tourist attraction but a big event in the lives of a handful of residents who toiled all year to beat last year's prize winning red onions or the monster leek or the perfectly symmetrical dahlia. It was probably true to say that obsession was not as powerful as amongst some Northern allotment based societies but competition and rivalry was still intense. Very intense.

Into this boiling cauldron of local politics, envy and intrigue, were thrust our three musketeers. Apparently Marjorie was Assistant Vice Chair, or something like that, on the rather portentous sounding Port Isaac Horticultural Society Flower Show Sub Committee and as long ago as January when the Schedule was first decided Marjorie had volunteered a TV celebrity Garden Designer to judge the local spuds. At this point she didn't have a TV celebrity Garden Designer in mind. It was just that Mrs. Pumfret was so proud of having secured someone from BBC Cornwall's 'Radio Cookbook' to judge the jams that Marjorie simply had to retaliate. In a fit of blind pique she invented this celebrity but said she couldn't release his name, yet, for what she mysteriously described as 'contractual reasons'. Of course the Sub Committee were all agog and made their own mind up as to who it might be – including some garden presenters that had been dead for many years.

Marjorie fretted about her 'little white lie' for many weeks but when it came out in the published minutes that it was all signed, sealed and delivered but the celebrity couldn't be named for what the minute taker now called 'legal reasons' then she was committed. She simply had to find someone. She made some discreet enquiries through a contact in the Royal Horticultural Society and also phoned some of the television stations without success. She was horrified to discover some of the fees that even quite unknown 'celebrities' charged and, although some were willing to appear, they wouldn't under any circumstances judge the entries.

She was beginning to despair and wonder whether she should admit her guilt and resign from the Sub Committee, accepting any disgrace and humiliation that Mrs. Pumfret could inflict, when the propinquity of planning to redesign her garden occurred to her. Guy had told Johnny and Marjorie that he couldn't start before late summer. He explained that he made it a rule not to work over July and August except one year when he had appeared in a South TV garden show in a regular feature called Garden Surgery. Guy's job was to look at some withered rotten stick and say 'I think your ... (fill in relevant species or cultivar) is suffering from a slight case of DEATH.' Unknown to Guy he had just been firmly pencilled in (that's pencilled in as tentatively as, say, stone engraving) for the Port Isaac Horticultural Society Annual Show as TV celebrity gardener.

On the second week of Guy's work in Johnny and Marjorie's garden she tentatively dropped, very casually so it wouldn't break, a remark about how lovely it was to have such a renowned gardener in the village and how honoured and thrilled the local gardeners were. They were dying to meet him and wouldn't it be just perfect if he could spare the following Saturday afternoon for a tea and a slice of cake with the local Horticultural Society. Of course Guy accepted. But almost as soon as the acceptance was leaving his lips Marjorie continued her sentence, 'and judge a few plants and veg. Oh good I'm so pleased you've accepted.' And so the deed was done. Marjorie copied a photo off one of Guy's brochures and soon all the telegraph poles in the village had 'TV Gardener judges local show' daubed in large luminescent pink, orange and yellow letters. Actually Guy was flattered, even if he did overhear more than one person say something along the lines of 'Who's he? I've never heard of him. I think he must be on one of them Digital channels.'

On the morning of the show Guy had to mug up desperately on the rules and regulations. Apparently there were any number of arcane rules and unofficial tips about how to tie the top of your onions when they are displayed but none of this information was available in the published schedule. It seemed to Guy that it was unfair to judge a competition by rules that weren't clearly displayed when you enter. Bob even offered the useful observation, 'No wonder all the show entrants range from the elderly to the terminally anally retentive – no self-respecting teenager would find this sort of stuff cool.'

Maya had agreed to judge the children's entries and crafts. Guy and Bob had cringed with embarrassment when Marjorie had asked (or was it told) her. This was on two counts. Firstly they didn't know why being a woman should automatically qualify you to know all about children and crafts. Guy and Bob's assumption was that Maya hadn't got any children and apart from the natural monopoly on giving birth there was no other reason to assume that this predisposed her to childcare and crochet. The second was that Maya was an expert in a number of areas of horticulture and just as good if not better qualified to judge the plants and veg classes than Guy. She was far more knowledgeable than Guy on grasses, bamboos, water plants and marginals, plus a reasonable range of herbaceous plants, most areas of vegetables (particularly the more exotic and unusual ones) and could probably give Guy a run for his money on other plants. Guy was more of a traditional tree and shrub man and although he could separate (and pronounce correctly) obscure Japanese maples he would sometimes struggle to name recently introduced but reasonably common bedding plants. Nonetheless Maya seemed genuinely pleased to be asked to judge the children and crafts classes and readily agreed.

There was furious activity around the Port Isaac Village Hall all morning with cars full of plant materials jockeying for position in the narrow street. People would wait in the car with the engine running for 10 minutes, impatiently tutting and looking generally stressed, in order to get a slightly better parking spot. Guy couldn't understand why they didn't just abandon their cars at the end of the street and carry the plants back up the lane. There was one particularly ugly scene where someone drove forwards into a spot that someone had hoped to reverse into. They had got the boot open and were already starting to unload when the driver of the other car came up and tried to close the other one's boot. When they realised they were not going to deter the person from unloading, the frustrated driver waited until they thought no-one was looking and then crushed one or two odd petals from the floral displays. Not enough to be immediately noticeable but enough to spoil the symmetry of the blooms for any capable judge.

By 11 O'Clock all exhibitors were barred from the premises and all excuses and pleas for extra time ignored. Only committee members were allowed to remain. The doors were solemnly shut and locked with a huge mortice key and then rattled to double check. At 11.05 precisely after some coded knocking from one of the officials the door was warily reopened and the judges were ushered in. All but Maya. She was missing.

Strangely Marjorie was not in the slightest perturbed by Maya's absence. Apparently each judge gets allocated a minder, someone to record the results and answer any questions. Marjorie had made sure that she was allocated to Guy. On the other hand Mrs. Pumfret was practically apoplectic with anxiety. She was walking up and down outside the doors muttering to herself and putting her extremely tiny watch right up to her right eye. She normally wore glasses but refused to put them on for special occasions in case a photographer came from the local paper. She had once tried contact lenses but kept losing them, normally when she was making jam. In fact …the more Mrs. Pumfret seemed to be in distress the calmer and more serene Marjorie became.

13. Getting Wrecked

In the end Bob was coerced by Guy to judge the children's and crafts classes which he performed with customary perversity. He awarded top prize for the messiest stitched cushion with the most garish design on the grounds that whoever had made it probably needed cheering up. Sensible Show judges always make sure that they are out of town by the time the entrants get to see if they have won or not. But Bob obviously hadn't read the unwritten handbook of judge etiquette. He wanted to see one entrant in particular. It was an 11 year old girl who had produced a driftwood sculpture. She hadn't really added a lot or changed it – just stuck some goggle eyes and frizzy hair and a Gonzo style nose on it. What Bob was interested in was where she had got the wood from. It was a lovely. A large, piece of curved and bleached wood. Oak, Bob thought, but it was so old and weathered he couldn't be sure.

He found his victim, congratulated her on her 1st prize in the "Monsters and Freaks" category. This wasn't much of an honour as she was the only entrant. Then he popped the question about where she had had found the wood explaining that he had been searching in all the bays roundabout and hadn't managed to find anything other than plastic.

'I bought it in a shop in Boscastle. There's no point waiting around on the beach for it. You either find nothing or it's like the other year when that timber ship sank – you couldn't move on the beach for people backing their trailers up to take bits of two by two.'

'Has the shop got any more?'

'Yeah, some. Charge you an arm and a leg for it though. The trick is to stop them prettifying it. They mostly use it to frame mirrors or paint dolphins on it but there's usually a few bits at the back of the shop they haven't done anything with yet. Doesn't come from Cornwall though. The guy buys it from somewhere in England. You know across the Tamar that is. Do I get a commission?'

'I've already given you that. I judged the classes. I think there were some cash prizes for the kid's entries weren't there?'

'Not so as you'd notice. I don't think I'll be able to buy an evening out or even a decent eyeliner for 50p. I guess it must have been a lot of money when you were around.'

Bob wasn't quite ready to be considered no longer 'around' but took his imminent non-existence as an excuse to cut short this fascinating conversation on fiscal inflation to make all haste for Boscastle before the shops shut. Still no longer driving, Guy had to drop him off. Guy didn't want to stay but promised to come back in an hour or two.

Bob found the shop quickly – it was on the tidal stretch of the river on the path leading down to the harbour with its 'blowhole' where the lapping waves on the other side of the hill are squeezed into a narrow crevice and then expelled with whalelike enthusiasm outside of the harbour wall. He quickly selected some pieces, negotiating a 'trade discount', and stacked these outside a conveniently situated pub to wait for Guy's return.

'Oh alright, just the one then,' he said to no-one particular as he entered the dark recesses of the pub and surveyed the tempting array of local brews. After straining to read the Original Gravity ratings of each tap he eventually put the young Australian barman out of his misery by ordering the guest ale known as 'Smuggler's Ale'. Bob remembered tasting this once before in an almost forgotten early teenage trip with his Uncle's family to visit St. Michael's Mount. At the time the half glass of his Aunt's pint he was offered was an illicit pleasure matching the illegality of its name. Although you can walk over to St Michael's Mount at low tide they had gone over by boat. It seemed a long way to the young seafarer and enough for him to work up a thirst. He had downed his coke and was pleading for more drink. The restaurant had just stopped serving and his Aunt, who was generally more soft-hearted than his Uncle or his cousins when it came to parting with any food or drink, allowed him some. She argued it would mix with the soft drink and make a sort of shandy. Unfortunately it was fairly strong and Bob followed a fit of uncontrollable giggling with falling into the sea off the harbour wall. By this time the tide had started to turn and Bob was lucky not to break his spine by landing in the shallow water. Happy days.

There was something about being at the seaside that brought out the little boy in Bob. He was musing on fishing for blennies in rock pools and building elaborate sand castles that grew and grew in complexity and layout until the tide came to destroy the city like some giant Tsunami. He was pretty much lost in his own thoughts as two red faced fishermen settled into the snug behind him.

They were muttering something about Bass and Mackerel and the difference between the sea fishing trips they did and rock fishing for Wrasse or baiting various kinds of flatfish in the estuaries. They started berating one of the local dealers and what he'd asked them to bring in and when. Contrary to Bob's expectation the discussion was never about the fishing issues that made the news (falling stocks, EU regulations, French and Spanish trawlers) but what the outsider might consider the little things (judging the amount of fuel, what the weather was going to do in a particular stretch of water, whether to sacrifice speed by leaving redundant backup equipment on shore). These were the issues which would make the trip economical or not and safe or not. Most of them had given up on the bureaucrats long ago. They were just a natural risk like a high swell to be endured. You might hate them but hating them wouldn't make any difference and so they just got on with the things they could control or influence.

Bob's attention switched to his fish pie. He wondered what was in it. He could identify the Salmon which he thought strange to find in a fishing port. The fish was pale and pretty obviously fish farmed rather than caught in the wild. There was something that looked like cod but was a great deal tastier. This was probably one of the unfashionable fish that would never sell in a restaurant or fish and chip shop but was just as good if not better than cod, plaice or haddock. There was another white fish as well. Pollock? Who knows? The secret to a good fish pie is that it doesn't matter what the fish is as long as it is fresh. It shouldn't be used as an excuse for getting rid of grey slimy, bony, offcuts that had been in the freezer for a month. This pie was what you would expect. Although the fish could easily have come from the south coast into one of the local resellers it was definitely good and fresh. Bob had a reputation with Guy and Maya of always being the first to finish his meal, no matter how tongue-searingly hot. He made short work of the pie which, although being 50% potato, still came with a mountain of chips. Maya would always complain if meals came with two carbohydrates. As a vegetarian she tended to be on the receiving end of meals in which rice or pasta would be the main ingredient and potato or garlic bread as the supporting act. This perplexed her greatly and she used to complain about the 'fish and chip' culture of the UK in which you had a choice of the carbohydrate plus meat or fish based protein element or the carbohydrate on its own. As a grower of a bewilderingly exotic palate of oriental and western fruit and vegetables she simply could not understand the British addiction to the bland South American potato in which the taste of grease, or fish obscured by grease, came as the most interesting element. Unless drowned in salt and vinegar of course.

Bob, on the other hand, leaned back expansively in his chair, with a bloated belly and Cheshire Cat grin. He had left the vegetables (just peas) on his plate as too fiddly to bother with and was deeply content. He tended to think that peas and the knife and fork were not really designed to go together and didn't follow Winnie the Pooh's strategy of eating his peas with honey, 'it makes my peas taste funny, but it keeps them on my knife'.

He tuned in again to the Fishermen's conversation. They were talking about some catch that someone had brought in late last night.

'Derek was really put out. Said it cost him a day's fishing bringing in that body to where the Coastguard could arrange for it to be winched into the helicopter. Reckoned it was some illegal immigrant, not a holiday maker. 'Course the sea had bloated the body up, rocks smashed in the head. Pretty gruesome as usual.'

Bob was straight out of the door before he heard any more and on the phone to Guy.

14. Headless Chicken

Guy was swiftly round to Boscastle to pick up Bob. Even in their haste Guy and Bob loaded the driftwood which was still exactly where Bob had left it. Then they looked at each other as if to say, 'What now?' They decided to ring the Coastguard. The guy on watch didn't seem to be familiar with whatever the Fishermen had found and was going down the line of implying that the fishermen were just winding the tourists up and in any case they could be referring to something that occurred years ago. He went off to contact the regional HQ to see if he could find anything out about it but made it quite clear to Guy that he shouldn't have any expectations of them getting back with any meaningful information.

Guy insisted on going in to the pub and speaking to the fishermen to get more details. It seemed the obvious and simple thing to do and wondered why Bob hadn't done the same. Perhaps he should have done because the fishermen were nowhere to be seen. Presumably they were regulars and would be well known. They asked the bar staff. Unfortunately the bar staff were not regulars. The younger bloke on the bar was very helpful: in tone at least. But it turned out that both the staff working that day were fresh from University in Australia and were just working their way through the holidays. They didn't yet know which of their customers was a year-round regular, a second home owner, or a one week tourist. They were still grappling with the mental arithmetic involved in taking the orders and trying to understand the UK accent and idioms. They implied, albeit politely, that it wasn't really their job to recognise the customers and find out their names or where they lived. The infuriating thing was that they were right. Whereas someone entering the pub would have a fifty-fifty chance of remembering the bar staff if they saw them again, the same was not true for anyone serving the customers. Unless they were the kind of regular that propped up the bar and told you their life story or had the sort of hideous physical deformity that you couldn't help but stare at (preferably having three heads or green skin). Otherwise it was highly unlikely that they would be able to recall them but they did recommend speaking to the shift co-ordinator as she was local. She was renting a place from someone called Kevin Ladher and the address was half way along Paradise Road at the top of the village.

Bob thought it was just an effort on the part of the bar staff to get rid of them but they went anyway in search of this Kevin. Bob rang the bell but couldn't hear it ring so banged loudly on the door. There was no reply. He waited, tried looking in a few windows and round the back. Nothing in sight. There was someone watching though. Bob could feel it or thought he could. He tried knocking next door to see if they knew when their neighbour might be back. There was no-one there either. 'Holiday cottage I expect' he muttered to himself and walked back down the drive to rejoin Guy who was just trying the Coastguard again.

In the road there was a heavily pregnant lady who had just arrived by car and was taking out some shopping. 'Here let me help you with that,' Guy volunteered. 'No that's okay' she said, 'the arms still work and I need the exercise'. Then he heard someone shouting, 'Ursell, get in here!' The lady threw her eyes heavenwards and then said, 'Actually you can help me with these, and the name is Flo – he just calls me that when he's drunk or mad. I think it's his old girlfriend. She went off to become a nurse in Exeter ages ago.' She looked at him conspiratorially, gave him the bags and then linked arms with him. Bob helped her to the house he had just been knocking at the door of – the second one that is. He waited at the door for her to open it but she said, 'that's alright just leave them there'. He asked her if she knew of someone next door called Kevin Ladher. 'No, there's no-one next door by that name. He doesn't live there.' There something sad about the way she said it as if she would like to say more but 'you'd better go now' was all she would add.

Meanwhile Guy, on the recommendation of the Coastguard HQ, had decided to ring the local Police. The Police were not very helpful either. They asked Guy a lot of questions about himself, checked him up on the computer; asked him what business it was of his, asked him about Maya, asked what his relationship was with Maya, asked him what they thought they could do about it, people go missing all the time, was she an illegal immigrant and so on and so on. By the time Guy came off the phone he felt like he was the criminal. He wasn't quite sure what he'd done but probably wasting police time at the very least. He was also irritated by the fact that they assumed Maya wasn't a British citizen. Guy didn't know whether she was or not but his assumption had been that she was – her English was too good to have arrived recently. She had probably been in the country for a long, long time, perhaps from birth, if the way she spoke could be taken as a reliable indicator.

As the Police didn't seem to be very interested Guy and Bob decided to head back into Port Isaac and see if they could speak to the local RNLI or Coastguard station again.

As they were driving back in (and just before their mobile signal was about to disappear because of the intermittent local coverage) they got a call back from the Coastguard saying that they had a report from shore of something floating off the coast of Port Quinn. A helicopter had been dispatched from RAF St. Mawgan. They reported no-one visible in the sea but there were some objects floating presumably dumped from a passing boat. It was decided to send out a lifeboat to investigate the objects. The boat was coming out of Padstow, where they had a bigger vessel, rather than Port Isaac. The Coastguard wasn't at all sure it was connected but thought they ought to know. He said there had been no reports of any bodies being discovered in the last 24 hours.

The casualness of the Coastguard and the shortness of the timeframe they had limited their comments to had rather surprised Guy. When he enquired he was told that they normally recover half a dozen bodies in a season – the last was a family. A father and two sons had got into difficulty with what the Coastguard called a rip tide on a seemingly safe open beach. The elder son tried to help the younger, the father tried to help both of them but they were quickly swept into high swelling seas and smashed against adjacent rocks. The eldest son was said to be a strong swimmer – in a swimming pool that is. It was difficult for Guy to believe that something so beautiful as the sea off the Cornish coast could also be so deadly for the unwary, the unprepared or the plain unlucky.

Guy could not concentrate on finishing off any work that day on the garden and so he decided to try and check out anywhere that Maya might have gone. He knew it was probably useless and probably better to stay where they could be contacted (as he was totally unsure from recent experience of where he could be guaranteed to be available on the mobile phone network) but both Guy and Bob felt the need to be doing something. They went first along the coast path to the north of Port Isaac but only for about a mile before turning back and retracing their steps part of the way. They couldn't see anything out to sea or on land. They then explored the valley up towards the overland footpath to Port Quin but after going half the way decided to turn back and follow the road to St. Endellion Church.

They found nothing and the last impudent marmalade fingers of the setting sun were spreading sensuously over the dark folding hills. It was time to head back into the village.

As Guy came over the rise to head back down Church Hill his mobile rang. It was a voicemail message from the Police. He was to call them straightaway. He called them straightaway. They wanted to know where he was. He told them. They wanted to interview him straightaway. He was to stay exactly where he was. They would send a car. They wouldn't say why.

Half an hour later, in pitch darkness, a Police car was seen cruising the houses at the bottom of the hill. Guy and Bob walked down and attracted their attention.

Guy was cold, tired and fed up. Bob was okay. He was resigned to waiting and reserving any nervous energy for whatever needed to be done. But Guy was rather irritable and was a little short with the young Policeman.

'What's happened? Have you found her? We've been waiting half an hour for you. You could have picked us up at the B&B. We could have got changed and got something to drink. Have you found Maya for God's sake?'

'Sorry sir. Is Maya the lady you reported missing?'

'Yes, man. Have you found her?'

'Er, no, sir. It's something else. At least I hope it is.'

'What are you talking about?'

'Er, perhaps you'd like to step into the car sir?'

'What the hell is it?' Guy, despite himself, was beginning to shout and become hysterical.

'Just step into the car sir.' The oliceman was now being a little more assertive and had his flat palm firmly behind Guy's back.

Bob just nodded at Guy to get on with it and do it. Guy obliged. Bob asked if he was wanted as well. No was the answer. He just had to leave his name, home address and where he was staying. They would be in touch if necessary.

Guy was driven to a local police station. The Policeman kept talking to him, became quite chatty, but never told him what had happened. He was to see some special investigator. It wasn't a uniform job, the Policeman said, but he would be at the interview and would make sure Guy got a cup of tea. The answer to peace in our time – the offer of a cup of tea. Strangely that was exactly what Guy wanted. He was now too exhausted to be confrontational. He just wanted to have a cup of tea and to be told what was going on.

'The time is 21:43. Interview with Guy Adamson. PC Plucknett and investigations officer J Parton present. Now then – please say your name for the benefit of the tape.'

'Guy Adamson.'

'This is not a formal interview at this stage but we like to get everything recorded these days. Saves time.'

'And trouble', added PC Plucknett.

'Yes, thank you,' the officer continued, indicating by his scornful look that PC Plucknett should reserve his contributions to the tea making department. 'We'd like you to tell us, in your own words, why you contacted the Coastguard earlier.'

'That's not a crime is it?'

'Oh no, we just wanted to know what it was, in your own words, that you were looking for and why?'

'I would have thought that was perfectly obvious,' the exasperated Guy sighed. 'We…'

'Excuse me, for the benefit of the tape can you say who "we" is?'

'I'm a garden designer. Bob Conan, Maya Mei and I were in Cornwall to implement a new design for Johnny and Marjorie Stern's garden in Port Isaac. We had been working for a couple of weeks when Maya disappeared.'

'A couple of weeks? I thought you chaps came in and did it over a weekend while the wife was away.'

'That's television. We produce a quality design in close collaboration with the owner, with local materials and plants that will evolve gradually season after season … and besides, Bob hurt his arm and we were distracted by a local Flower Show and well, it just overran. I'd budgeted for two weeks but it looks like it's going to take us at least three. Anyway that's irrelevant. Maya went off for a walk – we think north from Port Isaac on the coast path yesterday. She hasn't been seen since.'

'What makes you think she isn't off in some guest house being bonked silly?'

'I hope she is – I really hope she is. No. It's not like her. In the short time I've got to know a little about her I know she would let us know where she was if it was at all possible. We gave her a mobile phone. That reminds me. She had an unpleasant encounter with one of the farmers on the headland. Near St. Endellion I think. It was nothing much but it frightened her so we gave her the phone and asked her to let us know where she was.'

'What's that got to do with the Coastguard?'

'Nothing. I just thought…'

'Why did you phone the Coastguard?' Mr Parton interrupted.

'Bob overheard two fishermen speaking in a pub in Boscastle.'

PC Plucknett rolled his eyes at Mr Parton but kept quiet.

'They said they had heard of someone bringing in a strange catch. I'm afraid I don't remember the details. You'll have to ask Bob. The important thing is that there was something about what they said that made him think of Maya. We were worried that maybe she had slipped and fell on the coast path, or worse, that she may have fallen into the sea or onto the rocks.'

'So she could have been dead for at least 24 hours.'

'I, er, suppose so.'

PC Plucknett broke his silence. 'Bodies can bloat up and get smashed pretty quick in this surf but I reckon that puts her out of the frame.'

'Have you got anything more to add Mr Adamson?'

'No, not really.'

'Either you have or you haven't.'

'No I haven't.'

'Good.'

'Only I want to know why you've brought me here?'

'You didn't see anything from the shore then?'

'No. We went out on the path but there was nothing. We don't even know for sure that she went that way.'

'Okay. I suppose we owe you some sort of explanation. The truth is we have found something today. Quite a lot of somethings. But just bits. The PC here, who is a bit more familiar with these things than I am, reckons they're unusual and well, bits of animals. Not human at all. But I'd be obliged if you'd keep this to yourself. Same as the Coastguard. We've asked him not to say anything either, until the parts have been analysed and sorted and we can make some sort of statement to the press that isn't likely to send all the cat and dog owners in the area into a fit of panic. Investigations are ongoing you might say. What I can say is that your friend is more likely to be in the local guesthouse than the sea. The PC here reckons these bits of bodies rotted on land before they were thrown out to sea.'

'They are definitely animal? Not human?'

'Animals. Exotic he reckons. Cut up. Bloated and half eaten body parts. Headless. Pointless. Senseless.' Mr Parton stared at the wall over Guy's shoulder, unable to make eye contact. His eyes appeared to be clouded over with whatever stomach churning visions he remembered. 'There was an unidentified woman found a few weeks back but that's not our job. It was the same stretch of coast but she could have drifted in from anywhere. I think they said she was of Chinese extraction.'

'Probably thought there were cockles in the bay' interrupted PC Plucknett. Parton stared furiously at him and then asked Guy, 'How well did you say you knew this girl who's missing?'

'I only met her a few weeks ago. She has some excellent references and she's been invaluable.'

'What nationality is she?'

'I'm afraid I never asked. I just assumed she's British.'

'My boss always says *assume* makes an *ass* out of *u* and *me* but then he *is* an ass. Nonetheless I'd like to see those references.'

'I left them back in Dorset but I could get the Agricultural College she studied at to fax or email them through again.'

'If you could. The PC will give you the local station details. He'll send them on to us.'

'Excuse me, who is "us", if you don't mind me asking?' Guy almost added, 'for the benefit of the tape' but decided not to.

'Didn't I say? Her Majesty's Customs and Excise.'

15. Paws for Reflection

Bob was still waiting for Guy when he got in late to the B&B. Guy explained how the conversation had gone. As far as Guy was concerned he was getting no help from the Police over Maya but he recognised that missing persons was very rarely something that the police could help with unless they could associate it with a crime or a young person at some sort of risk. Maya, being in her twenties, was not considered young. Neither was it a potential 'crime', and Guy was at a loss to think what 'crime' it might be. PC Plucknett had been quite friendly after the interview and tried to set Guy's mind at rest. He suggested that she would probably just turn up but they would add her to a register available to all officers just in case. At any rate Guy was now dog tired, more from nervous exhaustion than physical effort, and agreed to reconvene with Bob in the morning. Guy's head was spinning and he knew he would be unable to come up with a plan, cunning or otherwise, in his current state of mind.

Guy slept longer than Bob and found him already on site.

'Ah, the one armed bandit. I don't know what you expect to do to get this garden finished.'

'I had a phone conversation with the consultant in Exeter earlier. She's quite optimistic that I can start light work again next week.'

'Next week! I was hoping to be gone a week ago. Anyway never mind that. It's not important anymore. I'm not sure we can finish it at all.'

Unknown to them Johnny had come out into the garden and was breathing in the fresh seaside air. 'What are you talking about? What's the problem?'

So Guy went through the whole sorry tale of Maya's disappearance. Strangely Johnny was greatly affected by anxiety for Maya. It seems, from a standing start of open hostility, via a grudging respect, that Johnny had become rather taken with Maya.

'What we need is an action plan' he said, striking a pose with one foot forward and hand on hip. He looked rather like Montgomery prior to a desert battle as he began to rattle off a series of suggestions. Some of these were faintly ludicrous, for example abseiling down the adjacent cliffs to examine the rocks for clues, but others made a good deal of sense. They would speak to the Fore Street shop owners, pub and hotel staff, with a description of Maya, to see if anyone remembered seeing her and where she might have been going when she disappeared. Once the information was gathered they could set out, a few metres apart if necessary, and look for her or for evidence of where she might have been. They would also contact the referees given on the CV she had submitted to Guy to try and get family details to see if her relatives or friends had been called by her – but without trying to alarm them, which would probably be pretty difficult to strike the right balance. In short they would try all the normal routes to trace a missing person presumed okay. It was late morning by the time they had reconvened and shared their findings. This didn't take long. There was not a lot. She had been seen by the owner of one shop heading in the direction of the coast path. They were still waiting for her family details from the Agricultural College in order to contact them. Needless to say there was a lot of conversation, explanation and proof for Guy to go through even though the College did have a record of sending him the information before.

Undaunted, Johnny organised a few of his drinking pals (some with hip flasks, some with supermarket carry-outs, some definitely on the wagon and not a moment too soon) into a Sheriff's posse. With Bob and Guy they made a striking silhouette on the Port Isaac skyline with fifteen evenly spread people walking out on the high field above the bay as if herding Longhorns instead of slightly intimidating the half dozen Friesian cows. If only they had six-shooters instead of Tesco carrier bags!

There was a great deal of shouting and noise with Johnny pacing up and down the line making sure that people didn't get too close together or lose their line. Guy was next to Bob who deliberately took the lowest line nearest the sea. He didn't want any of the more intoxicated participants taking a tumble. Everyone concentrated really hard and it wasn't long before they started to pick up potential clues: a man's comb, a discarded banana peel, a broken dog's lead and so on. Unfortunately none of them could be associated with Maya in any way but everything was bagged and a note made of where it was found.

After about a mile and a half some of the less hardy began to make their excuses. Weak bladders, couldn't climb the next hill and, Bob's favourite, 'just remembered I've left a nude model in the studio and I promised to make them some peanut butter and jelly sandwiches'. They still had 6 people though – enough to do the job reasonably well as it was unlikely anyone would stray very far to either side of the coast path. Johnny and Marjorie were there plus there were a couple of indomitable ladies from Trelights, Rene and Joy, that we're friends of Marjorie from some local society or other called the Tuesday Girls. 'Because we meet on Tuesdays', they would chime in unison without being asked to explain the name of their club and then collapse in a fit of giggles as if it were the funniest joke ever.

Collectively they all decided to make a brief pause around some rocks at the top of one of the hills. Fortunately Rene and Joy had brought a flask of tea and various other useful survival rations. Guy was sure that if he asked them nicely if they had anything for taking stones out of horses' hooves they would both have swivelled on their brogues and produced two Swiss army knives in instant unison.

But Johnny was restless. He couldn't sit on the flat rocks and continued pacing up and down the headland. Suddenly he shot off inland, over a barbed wire fence, in the direction of a farmer's barn.

Guy, also, was beginning to look more worried. Going out with a search party like this made him realise, probably for the first time, that Maya may well have fallen and hurt herself. He felt somehow responsible. He should have been with her. He should have taken more care of her – as an employer, as a friend, as a fellow human. He should have been less foolish than to just wait and see, in the hope that everything would turn out alright in the end. He also shouldn't have been so foolish as to put his faith in some geriatric thespian to sort everything out for him!

One look at Bob's face and Guy knew that he must be feeling something pretty similar. Having gone out on the headland like this and experienced the futility of looking for a needle in a haystack brought it home to both of them how powerless they were to change anything past. Whatever had happened to Maya they could not protect her.

Bob did understand Guy's concern, and shared it, but he didn't share his guilt. When they got talking about it Bob found Guy's attitude rather patronising and told him so. 'What makes you think you are responsible for any other human being? Okay – you're an employer and you have some legal obligations but they really relate to the workplace so unless she's been sawn in half with a hedge trimmer you're okay.'

Guy winced.

'Listen', Bob continued, 'she's a fully grown up adult. Don't think that, because she's a woman and smaller than you, that you have some special duty to protect her. That's the worst kind of chauvinism.'

'It's not that. I would do the same for anyone. I don't think it's because she is smaller or weaker or very young. I hope it would be exactly the same if it was you or I. That's just common humanity.' Nonetheless Bob had clearly touched a nerve. Guy was not only feeling guilty. He was now feeling guilty about feeling guilty.

Johnny then re-emerged from over one of the stone walls. He was surprisingly lithe and athletic for an ancient alcoholic thespian.

He came up to the group and spluttered, 'I think I've cracked the case.' He produced a mobile phone. It wouldn't switch on when Guy tried it but he identified it as the one that had been given to Maya. 'Aha', said Johnny. Guy thought he was going to put his hands on his hips again in that Montgomery on the eve of battle pose. Johnny nearly did and then rather self-consciously moved his hands down and put them into his pockets, took them out again and let them dangle.

'Where did you find it?'

'Up at that barn over the field. I remembered once sheltering there when Marjorie and I got caught out on a walk when it pissed … sorry… when it precipitated rather forthrightly in a vertical manner.'

'Show me', commanded Guy.

Johnny, Bob and Guy climbed over the wall. Marjorie and the ladies sensibly opened the gate which was only a few yards to the left. They walked rapidly up to the barn. Guy was first there and spread his arms to stop the others entering. 'I know it seems silly but can I go in on my own with Johnny please? In case there are any clues we don't want to trample all over the place.'

'You mean in case she's in there and you don't want the ladies to be upset?' Bob cruelly supposed.

'I don't imagine for a moment she's there but if she is I'll be the one wailing like a little girl. I'm sure the ladies would be very sensible and practical', snapped Guy.

Johnny showed Guy where he had picked up the mobile. It had been resting on straw and there was nothing particularly revealing there. No stains, no clothes fibres, no human hair: nothing. Not that could be readily seen anyway. Guy had a look around. He saw the swinging mechanism for the loft door. He looked around where anyone coming in that way might have been. There was compaction in the straw and the signs of an object being dragged but nothing particularly unusual in that. There were several sacks stacked up against the side wall that could easily have explained that. Johnny stayed by the door as if to keep the rest back. They constantly asked Guy what he could see and Guy pretty much ignored them.

Disheartened, he turned back towards them and gave a brief description of the layout. He had seen nothing of interest but he didn't want them to go in anyway. There were some rusting, but still lethal, bits of harrows, scythes and so on that he didn't want anyone to tread on or fall accidentally onto. The others resented being treated as children but had no particular desire to go in to the slightly gloomy interior.

Guy now started to circle the barn. He could see deep tyre tracks. A tractor no doubt. He could also see some lighter but definite tracks. A Land Rover or perhaps one of those open backed 4x4 trucks. All of the tracks led direct from the field entrance to the barn except one. That set was fairly fresh and led direct to the other side of the field. Guy followed it. The tracks led direct to a wall and just stopped. The wall was too high to see over as the ground dipped in front of it. Guy had to walk along to where the ground was higher and then start to climb over. It was difficult because it was a dry stone wall and the top stones would come loose if you put too much weight on them. Eventually Guy rested his stomach and body weight along the length of the top of the wall and flopped over to the other side, landing unceremoniously on his backside in the mud.

In front of him was a wide open stretch of freshly ploughed earth. The field was swarming with seagulls. Guy was surprised they hadn't flown up in a noisy swarm in response to his arrival. Instead they continued busying themselves feasting on leatherjackets and grubs. The nearest ones to him merely leered with their heads on one side before returning to their task. There was the sound of a tractor but from Guy's prostrate viewpoint it was well out of sight over a curve in the horizon. The farmer was obviously still ploughing. Guy got up, looked closely down at the earth and then half walked, half ran, hunched up and crouching, along the base of the wall. He wanted to reach the point at which the tracks stopped on the other side.

He found a point which must have roughly corresponded to where the field on the other side dipped. Unfortunately anything that might have been seen, and Guy was by no means sure what he was hoping to see, was well and truly ploughed up.

After a few moments of indecision the sound of the tractor started to become louder and louder. It must have reached the far side of the field and was coming back around the perimeter. Guy ran along the wall, this time towards the coast path. He could see a low fence at the end which would be easier and quicker to get over than to go back over the wall. He didn't look back to see whether the farmer saw him. He just ran.

Once on the coast path he walked a little to the right so that the corner of the wall obscured him and he had chance to recover his breath. Why had he run? He tried to tell himself that he was trespassing and that farmers can often get very upset about that. But there was more to it than that.

The sound of the tractor continued to get nearer and nearer until it seemed to be directly on top of him. Then it suddenly veered off and was gone back towards the lane on the landward side of the field.

16. Endellienta's Challenge

Guy looked down the coast path. At this point it rounded a cove on the opposite side of which was a small cave. He would have missed it if it hadn't been marked out by short poles connected by some sort of tape. In and out of the cave were coming what looked like spacemen. They wore white suits and big bubble helmets.

As he approached, none of them looked up. They continued to go in with empty bin bags and bring out full ones. Guy was virtually on top of them when someone challenged him.

'I'm afraid this part of the path is temporarily closed.'

'I can see that. I want to know why.'

'There are notices posted up at all the Tourist Information offices.'

'That doesn't answer my question.'

'It's closed. I'm afraid you must go back the way you came. We're very sorry for any inconvenience. We have to carry out some work for the environmental health department. The path should reopen in a few hours.'

'Why have you got police incident tape up then?'

One of the other men approached the barrier. 'Afternoon Mr. Adamson.'

It was the same officer that Guy had seen at the police station. The one that had turned out to be from HM Customs and Excise.

'Anything in those bags I should know about?' Guy asked.

'I don't think so. I trained as a zoologist but frankly I think we're going to need a forensic scientist to sort this lot out. My educated guess would be that we have bits of Humphead Wrasse, Asian Elephant, Irrawaddy Dolphin, Great White Shark, Leaf Tailed Gecko and Yellow Crested Cockatoo. The latter two are the only ones we found in anything approaching a state of readily identifiable wholeness. Apart from the Tiger that is.'

'What?'

'Yeah. We couldn't get at the others until we sorted out the tiger. Unfortunately she was so weak I think we killed her with the tranquilliser. I'm waiting to hear back from the guy at Newquay zoo.'

A look of slow recognition began to pass across Guy's face. Seeing it the officer looked at him more intensely. 'There is something you didn't tell me isn't there? You are involved.'

'There is something I didn't tell you because you didn't ask me and because I didn't know it was relevant.'

'Well…?'

'The other person I'm working with is called Bob. He went for a walk along the coast path the other day. I didn't know where, but I now know…at least I'm pretty sure… that it was here. He fell through some loose turf into what he described as some sort of cave but it was so dark he couldn't describe it. He broke his wrist, which was what we were worried about, but he also came back with some pretty viscous scratches and was babbling about funny sounds and smells. I think he must have been here.'

'So you think the Tiger was being used as some sort of guard dog? Not a very effective one though if that's the case. She was chained up and half starved. Bit of a shame really as there was meat all over the place just out of reach. Tigers don't scratch. They rip you apart. I'd wager it was more likely to have been some sharp rocks or a real guard dog.'

'Then why the Tiger?'

'I really don't know. They're worth more dead than alive and a lot less trouble. Anything from $50,000. It's an Amu. You may know it as the Siberian Tiger. I can only assume it was a "steal to order" commission from some rich eccentric in England who wanted it alive. The body parts usually trade in the Russian Far East on the Chinese border. I once met a guy at a conference who worked in the port of Slavyanka just 10 miles from the Chinese border. He led an anti-poaching unit and was a former lieutenant-colonel in the Russian Special Forces. Let's just say they take a rather more robust approach to international poachers than we do. The problem is the middle men and the end customers. You just can't get any support from the courts to come down hard on them. Worldwide that is, not just Russia and China. If you finger some local politician doing favours and turning a blind eye to illegal trade for the sake of owning a tiger skin the best you can hope for is a small fine. They don't even get sacked from office. As the tigers get rarer and closer to extinction the problem just gets worse. The trade becomes more profitable and, for law enforcement personnel on the ground, even more dangerous. Fortunately we're making some good strides with the Chinese government but it's difficult for them to treat enforcing regulations about Russian tigers as anything like a priority in their international trade plans. There are some wild animals that are poached but there is also an intensive breeding programme in China. Not a scientific breed and release programme. More like factory farming.'

'So it's the old red peril?'

'No, it has nothing to do with socialism or communism or any political, social or environmental policy as such. I guess capitalism, or whatever you want to call it, is older and more basic than that – it's about finding ways to feed your family by exchanging whatever you can get your hands on. From the days of the Silk Road the West has traded with the East regardless of beliefs or systems of government. It's a completely trans-national, apolitical and amoral. The people who buy, move and sell exotic animals are the same people that would be prepared to traffic in anything exotic – be it narcotics, armaments or people. They are just commodities. The greater the risk, the higher the price. They speak the universal language of greed. Apparently they don't trade officially in bones but admit to the wide-scale trading in skins from captive animals. We reckon there are about 5-6000 tigers in captivity in China kept for slaughter and trade. They use the skins for bribery and status gifts for corrupt officials. Sorry if that sounds a bit jaundiced. I've nothing against the Chinese government exclusively – like I say it's a global problem. The buyers create the trade both domestically and internationally.'

'I don't think you have to be polite for Maya's sake. I suspect she's got a pretty good handle on it – both good and bad, no matter how close or distant her cultural heritage is. I feel really guilty now I didn't find out more about her …and there am I talking about her in the past tense!' Guy swallowed and looked down. He turned his head to mask the welling tears and asked, 'I don't suppose there is any sign of…?'

'No. But we're not finished yet and so I'm going to have to ask you to leave.'

'You will call me if there is…?

'The police will doubtless be in touch. Yes.'

There was nothing much to do. Thankfully the stiff coastal breeze was atomising the lingering odour of filth and decay. Guy was more than happy to turn away and try and find Johnny and the rest.

He returned to a welcoming flask of hot tea and lots of questions, and some ginger biscuits. Guy disappointed them about the tracks leading up to the wall. There was nothing of interest to be seen on the other side. One of the ladies confirmed that the farmer who had ploughed the field was the same one that owned the barn. He was not much liked locally. Bit of a loner. He had come down from Yorkshire about 23 years ago they thought.

'Not long enough to be regarded as a local then' said Bob and was promptly dug in the ribs by Guy who interrupted by telling them about the cave. He couldn't remember the names of the animals that the Customs man had listed but he remembered to tell them about the Tiger. He then looked pointedly at Bob. Bob still looked blank. Guy had to prompt him.

'Tiger, tiger, burning bright, what immortal hand or eye can break your wrist and scratch your thigh?'

Bob was genuinely shocked when the realisation struck him. He realised how lucky he may have been. He had always been one of those people who are happy to take physical risks. When he was a youth he had been in a bad motorbike accident and had skidded along the road in his leathers, just got up and walked away from the mangled cars and written off bike. Since then he had regarded himself as virtually indestructible. But Guy could see Bob blanche at the notion of being that close to a desperate killer, knowing that in the dark cave a stumble to one side or the other could have made the difference between walking away and being lunched on limb by limb.

'The guy down there thinks it must have been a guard dog but they always make a lot of noise as well as take lumps out of you. I think you would have known it was a dog. My money is on a dying, sick Tiger who lashed out more out of instinct and pain than as a fit and able predatory hunter.'

The others kept asking Guy where he thought Maya might be. Guy confirmed that there was no evidence that she had been to the cave. He was quite emphatic with the group that she couldn't possibly have gone there but privately still wondered. Perhaps she had. Perhaps she was on her way from the cave. Perhaps she was on her way to the cave. If only he could remember what she had said last on that day but Guy had his head down concentrating on his work at the time. It could have been anything. He was sure she had mentioned St. Endellion or St. Endellienta but he couldn't remember what it was. She had certainly said something before about the saint having a godly way with animals. It was either by treating them kindly or possibly making sick ones well.

There was nothing to be gained by waiting at the coast. The party agreed to split up. By popular request Johnny had been persuaded to head for the nearest boozer in the hope of meeting some friends there. Bob, on the other hand, had the notion that they could somehow follow Maya's footsteps by trying to figure out what was in her mind. Bob and Guy set off for the church at St. Endellion to see if they could find out any more about this saint that Maya had become so enthusiastic about. It wasn't very hopeful but at least the activity stopped them from being burdened with too much unhealthy speculation.

It had just started to rain when the two caught sight of the grey blocked stone church tower of St. Endellion. The wind had got up and the sky was blackened and ominous. No theatrical thunder and lightning but enough to make the two of them run the last few hundred yards to shelter first under a set of conifers in the graveyard and then dash for the church porch. They shook the rain from their sleeves and jackets, shivering slightly as the temperature seemed to have dropped. Then they turned the heavy metal knocker to enter the church.

It was cool inside but, despite the onsetting gloom, it appeared light and airy. There was a cold elegance in the tall windows and even the wooden benches seemed comfortable to their wet and tired limbs. After a few moments quiet contemplation Guy got up to browse the tourist literature and read the plaques and inscriptions around the walls. The first thing to catch his eye was a tribute to the poet John Betjeman. He wasn't buried there – apparently he was buried in a nearby golf course, or rather the church of St. Enodoc at which he was buried, which was in turn half buried in the golf course by the drift of the sand dunes. The second thing he learned was the music. He wondered where he had heard the name Endellion before. He thought it sounded vaguely cultural and thought it was from a poem by Keats. But then he remembered *that* was Endymion and what he was really half-remembering was a CD he had by the Endellion String Quartet. Apparently their dim distant origins were originally connected to the village and the church still retained a distinguished classical music festival for which the event details were plastered around.

Then he came across his first reference to St. Endellienta. There was a shrine. It just looked to Guy like a small altar except that there was a family tree near it and someone had dropped a leaflet on the floor near one of the pews. Guy had seen a lot of village names from driving around during the last few weeks that were called Saint and abbreviated to St. this or St. that. They were all listed here as the names of the children of a Welsh king called Brychan. Guy assumed that this Brychan was a mythical figure – like Robin Hood and King Arthur – and that this family invasion represented some sort of cultural, military or religious invasion of early Christians from Wales. Nonetheless there was mention of an Ogham stone inscribed with his name implying that he was an actual person and that he was buried just outside the village at the crossroads on the road to Port Quin. Guy had already seen another Ogham stone in St. Kew inscribed in both Latin and Celtic. He knew these stones were unusual in Britain but common in Ireland. Perhaps these early Christian evangelical invaders were from Ireland or, more likely, shared a common Celtic culture spread across Ireland, Wales, Cornwall and Brittany.

This Endellienta, whether she existed in reality or fable, was said to have lead an exemplary, but totally humble, life tending a few cows. Unfortunately one of these strayed into a local lord's field and was slaughtered by him. Endellienta's uncle, who just happened to be King Arthur, killed the errant lord. Endellienta's miracle was not only to forgive the lord who had wronged her but also to bring him back to life. Guy dismissed the miracle and also the rather gratuitous connection with King Arthur but there was still something about the story that intrigued him. He wondered if Maya had reacted similarly – dismissing it superficially as harmless folk fantasy but surprised that this early society revered a) a woman, b) humility and c) forgiveness. What would Maya have done if she had come across this story? Would she have looked for other information? Bob suggested that she would have gone to try and find the Ogham stone and to read the inscription on it. So that's what they did next.

As they were walking out of the church door they virtually fell over the vicar from Port Isaac, Henry Ryol.

'Oh, are you the vicar of all the local churches?'

'Like the lady vicar in Boscastle you may have seen on a TV series a bit ago, most rural priests, including myself, have several churches to look after. St. Endellion is the central parish church for this area. But I'm not here for the parishioners. I was just telephoned and told to go the church and meet the Bishop here immediately. I suppose he thought choosing God's house was some sort of neutral territory.'

Bob blurted out something about bashing the Bishop being a popular occupation for young men. Henry didn't really understand but said that being summoned by the Bishop was rather like seeing the headmaster or getting the dreaded vote of confidence from a Football Club chairman. 'It appears I have been a very naughty boy and my job is probably in jeopardy although I haven't been quite as naughty as my beloved congregation thinks.'

'Just tell me it's none of my business but we had a friend who was most concerned when you were taken off by the police recently. I don't suppose you've seen her. She...'

The vicar interrupted 'I know who you mean. Maya. I have been telling her all about the local saints. She is a most able student. Far quicker to grasp the subtleties of ecumenical nuances than me I'm afraid. Perhaps if I'd paid attention to church politics and history a little more closely and not been distracted by gardening I wouldn't be in this predicament.'

'Sorry, what do you mean, gardening? And when did you last see Maya?'

'I haven't seen Maya for days. Not since I came up in your garden. I don't think she saw me though.'

'You have no idea where she might be?'

'Actually I do have a notion. Would you like me to mention it to the Police? I'm seeing them again after the Bishop, but not here. I didn't want the police to bump into the Bishop so I'm going to meet them down the road outside the Longcross Tavern.'

'Where? I mean where did you last see Maya?'

'I have no idea where. We got talking about farmers' cruelty to animals. I'm a vegetarian and it doesn't go down too well with the local farming community. I don't like fish either come to think of it. Anyway I mentioned a farmer called Penjerrick, who used to have a farm not far from St. Endellion. He had revived the ancient sport of bear baiting. I'm not sure where he is now, or even if the stories can be believed, but Maya became very agitated by the story I related. Maya told me she had been reading about a sister of Endellienta called Kew. When Kew asked to visit her brother he told her that she could only visit if she got rid of a bear. This was an excuse. The brother never expected his sister to take up the challenge. She did. She rid the village of the bear that had been plaguing them and the grateful villagers founded the church and named the village of St. Kew after her. Maya said that if she came across anyone doing anything like that she would put a stop to it and joked that maybe someone would name a village after her. I just thought it was the sort of thing young people say with no thought as to the possible consequences of meddling with unsavoury characters involved in a dangerous sport or criminal activity. But she told me that she had already had some sort of run in with farmer here. I wonder whether she was going back to confront him.'

'You should tell the police. You should tell them right now. Perhaps they already know who this person is and where they live.'

'Alright. I'll do that. Ah, here's the Bishop. I'll tell them right away as soon as I've seen the Bishop.'

Sensing the vicar's nervousness it was clear that Guy's and Bob's presence was not required for this interview. They made their farewells and headed down towards the place called Longcross to try to find the Ogham stone.

Bob was curious as to what trouble the vicar had got into and what was the meaning of what he was saying about gardening being his downfall? Guy smiled enigmatically. He wouldn't say anything other than 'I don't think he's going to have as much trouble with the Bishop as he thinks. I hear from the Horticultural Society that he's a bit of a champion carrot grower himself.'

17. A Longcross to Bear

It wasn't hard to find the stone. The place was called Longcross and there was a stone which had obviously been part of a "long cross" at some point. But as for reading the inscription it was no longer decipherable. The wind and rain of centuries had rendered it dumb. Whether it was an original piece of 5th or 6th Century Irish writing designed to leave cryptic messages indecipherable by the Romans or a later weather worn copy from a well-meaning antiquarian Guy couldn't make out. Seeing a hotel opposite with all day opening hours Bob encouraged Guy to accompany him for some refreshment with the promise and hope of finding out more about the stone.

Upon entering the bar their hearts sunk. There was Johnny and his cronies fighting what appeared to be a pitch battle over the cultural origins of curry. A family from Birmingham had got into a row with him about the "Balti belt" around the West Midlands and was arguing that curry was the British national dish. Johnny was having none of it. 'Tikka Massala is foreign muck – we want something British'. The scene was threatening to turn ugly as several chairs started to be brandished in the air. The bar staff appeared totally bewildered and neutral. One of them explained, 'I'm Irish, I just like the taste. You'd be doing me a favour if you broke that chair – everything's insured and we could do with persuading the owners to fund a refit.'

Guy and Bob decided to stay anyway. Perhaps they figured even a stormy port was still a port in a storm. Guy was still thinking about the far off time in history when the stone must have been carved and he wondered how the Celts would have argued with the Angles who would have argued with the Saxons who would have argued with the Romans who would have argued with the Phoenicians over what herbs and spices should or shouldn't be put with Cornish beef. How can people think we've become some sort of cosmopolitan melting pot over the last few decades when the truth is that we always were and certainly since the last Ice Age?

'Listen everybody,' Bob announced to the bar, 'if you want to beat seven shades of excrement out of each other you're welcome but be quick because I want several beers and a curry and the police and the clergy are going to be here any minute.'

Perhaps fearing that the scene could descend into some sort of chaotic cross between the Keystone cops and a vicars and tarts' party, the family from Birmingham decided to leave. Bob and Guy went to sit on their own but quick as a flash Johnny was over to join them.

'You're know you're completely and utterly wrong don't you?' asked Guy. 'Tikka Massala is about as foreign as Haggis. It's supposed to have been invented in Glasgow.'

'Yes it's just people from Birmingham I can't stand. They have such a whining accent.'

Fortunately lunch arrived and Johnny skulked back off to his new best friends behind the bar but not before relating a useful snippet of information. Guy had told him about the discovery at the cave partly to distract him from going off on another of his culinary or xenophobic rants. In response Johnny revealed that there had been an incident in the press a few years back during the 'mad cow' scare when the remains of 3 bears had been discovered in one of the destruction sites designated for cows. Although the site was a long way away, the animals had been traced back to a farmer in St. Endellion in North Cornwall. It was the same farmer that Guy had leaped over the coast path fence to avoid. But, according to Johnny, it was a different farmer to the one Maya had encountered. This farmer was late middle-aged and had always been single and lived alone.

Diggory Brae, on the other hand, had recently lost his wife in a car accident. The word in the village was that he had become slightly touched as a result. 'Fay' was the term they used. It seemed to convey anything from 'other worldly' to 'soft in the head'. But they were adamant that he was a good man and wouldn't hurt a fly.
But he had hurt his wife on that fatal occasion – that was the way he saw it. Diggory had been driving …and drinking. They say the accident wasn't his fault. An old person had suffered a heart attack, was driving the wrong way down a one way system and they met in a head on collision. But Diggory felt he would have been able to react much more quickly if he had been sober. There was an exit to one side which he had a second or two to take even though it might have meant spinning the driver side into the impact. He was breathalysed and lost his license. Since that day he hadn't touched a drop of alcohol and was riddled with remorse. But he had driven his farm machinery around out of economic necessity and had been known to occasionally take his Land Rover over the fields and one short stretch of road into the village. He had a daughter but, as far as Johnny knew, she had left him after the accident and gone to

live with her boyfriend in Newquay. That was what he had told people.

'So who is this other farmer, the one with the bears?' asked Guy.

'Penjerrick? The Police will have him on record, and all his known associates, because I think there was an incident where the RSPCA went round to check out an accusation and it turned nasty. He and a couple of others were arrested and Penjerrick was convicted for Grevious or Actual Bodily Harm or something similar. I'm not sure if they were just going to fine him but his performance in court earned him a few months in jail on top of the offence. I think the others got off because of some weak testimony on identification. Probably intimidated the witness.'

Guy was determined to make this connection to the police and have his farm searched. He kept popping out to the car park, and the road beyond, to spot the police when they arrived. The vicar arrived first, slightly ashen faced. He wouldn't say what the Bishop had said but it was clear that he had not been as jovial and understanding as Guy had expected. Guy bought him a drink. A brandy.

Eventually the police arrived. The constable was slightly surprised to see the vicar with alcohol in his hand as if he shouldn't drink (at least not on duty he thought). He encouraged the vicar to drink up and accompany him to his mobile interview room, a Ford Fiesta, but not before Guy had put his accusation about the bear baiting farmer. The constable was aware of the activity on the coast path and promised to contact them and see whether they were interested in an allegation of local bear baiting although he was rather dismissive of it having any basis in current reality as any previous offence was certainly before his time and he had been in the area station a couple of years.

By the time the vicar re-emerged Johnny and his companions had left. Guy and Bob were slumped in their seats in the bliss of being completely stuffed sideways. The vicar offered them another round. They accepted orange juice, which the vicar also ordered, and sat down to talk. They sat in silence for a while. Guy knew the drill. If the vicar wanted to talk, to confess, then silence was the best way to encourage him. If they talked about the weather or something similarly innocuous then nothing serious would ever be mentioned.

Two thirds of the way down his orange juice the beans were spilled. The vicar seemed to be a lot more upbeat now than when he had first arrived at the Tavern. He described how, when he had first arrived in the village, everyone was extremely kind and welcoming. There had been a brief interregnum between his arrival and the departure of the previous incumbent. He was left in no doubt that everyone was very pleased the post had been filled and that they were looking forward to his work in the parish. Slowly, almost imperceptibly, over the next three years his relationship with the village had crashed. He believed he was there to do good work, to help the needy and to bring a fresh conscience and awareness to the Christian community. The congregation, however, were not used to being told about starvation and education in the third world and how lucky and affluent they were to be in southern England or in Western Europe generally. They were used to regarding themselves as the economically dispossessed of southern non-England with a unique set of problems around seasonal trade, second home owners, road traffic, parking and European Union bureaucratic meddling. The vicar became actively involved in setting up a youth club in the Village Hall where youngsters could get together. In the vicar's mind this was to build the community of tomorrow where people could be engaged in physically active pursuits rather than be isolated in darkened bedrooms playing computer games. In the village's mind this was a hotbed of snooker, smoking and premature pregnancy. But worse was to come.

One poisonous curtain twitching pensioner who lived near the Hall became obsessed with the heterosexual and homosexual antics of the teenagers in the village and spread ugly rumours about the vicar's active involvement. This was Eskar Pronter's Dad, Ven, who had moved into the village to join him when Eskar's mother died. Henry and Eskar were already at loggerheads because Eskar's daughter Mormos was a budding singer but the vicar refused to let her perform in the Church. Henry regarded Eskar's daughter's image as profane, lewd for a sixteen year old and not suitable for a holy space. Admittedly this was largely based on the promotional posters she had glued to all the telegraph poles in the village which showed her in a skimpy t-shirt and ripped pair of fishnet stockings rolling a microphone provocatively on her inner thigh. Mormos tried to explain that this was symbolic of female emancipation in a fishing community but it made no sense to the traditionalist Ryol.

What actually happened to Ryol involved a couple of his favourite boys to which he was hoping to pass on his knowledge of the mysteries of giant vegetable growing. He had sworn them to secrecy over their mutual evening activities because he didn't want word to spread to his rivals at the Show (and also wanted to claim any Show awards for himself not share them with the boys). Every evening he would meet one or other of the boys and they would disappear off into dark corners of sheds and allotments. He had won a number of the highly coveted awards two years running. His expertise was humbling to his competitors and that ruthless competition seemed to have led to all sorts of slander and innuendo from friends and relatives of those who couldn't compete in the allotment. This was serious stuff. You don't laugh at the size of a man's parsnips and expect there to be no consequences.

So pride had come before his fall.

'But if that's all it is, jealousy, rumour and back-biting, then hopefully the Bishop dismissed it all as unbelievable or inconsequential nonsense?'

'No. Far from it. It's not the accusations of a few professional malcontents, it's a question of the trust of the church community and I no longer have it. Not just within the local area but within the church as a whole. Apparently Eskar told the Bishop of some previous indiscretion when I sought female company when my wife was dying. It was a long time ago and I was a bit of a mess at the time emotionally and spiritually. The Bishop was not at all sympathetic. He regarded my actions, then as now, as demonstrating a trend towards selfish disregard for those that needed my help and put their trust in me. I asked him if I could be moved to another parish but the Bishop said he has lined up some clerical job. I mean really clerical, dealing with parish records and general office duties, with a commensurate salary. He doesn't want me anywhere near the general congregation…anywhere, any place, any time.'

'But I don't understand. You're saying the boys were safe.'

'Well no, not really. That's the problem.'

'You mean they wouldn't testify on your behalf.'

'Oh yes, they'll testify. In fact they already have. When the police and then the church put the allegations to them, they thought they were doing me a favour by telling them everything. Fact is, I've been rather stupid and selfish and put them in great danger. That abandoned mine working that runs under Back Street from the church in the direction of the garden you were working in. It was too narrow for me to get through so I asked the boys to excavate it. I was looking for somewhere cold and dark to store equipment and also the vegetables for the night before the show. Then I realised the seam might run under my competitor's allotment and I couldn't resist asking the boys if they could dig upwards and try and pull the so-and-so's carrots and spuds right out from under him. It was stupid, I know. It was a bit of joke but they took me seriously so it was not just stupid in the end but a miracle they weren't seriously hurt. As it got nearer to the day of the show they decided they needed to make one last big effort to dig right through. But even with both of them down there they suddenly became terrified and disorientated in the dark when the torches started to fade. There was even a bit of a cave-in I understand. I put their lives at risk and it has now cost me my job.'

'Ah, that explains something,' said Guy, 'but how did Marjorie know?'

Bob looked at him quizzically. He wasn't in a position to understand the question, never mind speculate on the answer. 'Aren't you forgetting some small but important detail in all this?' he ventured.

'Yes, you're right,' answered both Guy and the vicar almost simultaneously. But they were thinking about completely different things. The vicar was thinking of how to rebuild his withered and slightly neglected faith in his calling and then rather wistfully about Marjorie Stern. Guy was thinking about his small but perfectly formed assistant.

18. Redemption and Judgement

Guy spent a restless night. He kept turning over and over in his bed. Maybe it was a little warm, maybe he had indigestion from a particularly lively Dhansak. Even if there was a physical trigger there was no doubt what occupied his mind. He began to conjure up all kinds of scenarios concerning Maya's absence. Guy wasn't normally prone to melodramatic fantasising or highly pessimistic speculation. He had tried to take a measured and calm approach figuring that, as he couldn't do anything about it, he would be better concentrating on things he could do. But tonight his imagination turned foetid and rank. He imagined murder, he imagined torture, he imagined rape. His mind boiled with anxiety.

In the end he threw off his bedclothes, decided to dress and go and sit in the lounge. This he did as quietly as possible, not wanting to wake anybody, and sat in the dark watching the blowing trees out in the small garden at the Bed and Breakfast. His mind was still working overtime but at least it was becoming a little more conscious and rational as the first glimmer of light started to come up over the horizon of the dark black Atlantic

Ocean. About half an hour before the rest of the household was due to rise he slunk back off to bed exhausted and numb.

He had slipped off into slumber but within what seemed like minutes he was dreaming again. There was a loud thumping. Everything seemed to be moving and vibrating. Someone was calling in the distance as if trying to retrieve a lost soul from the sea. He dreamed he was aboard a nineteenth century whaling vessel. The waves swelled in a force 8 gale. The spray swept straight over the tilting deck, smashing his face on the ship's rails before being tossed violently into the unforgiving depths. But someone was calling his name, calling him back. The waves kept beating on the side of the wooden ship with regular thumps. He struggled to surface in the cold black water but he could hear the caller getting louder. It was Mrs. Edwards, the lady who ran the Bed and Breakfast, and the side of the ship was his bedroom door.

With a sickening lurch into consciousness Guy asked her to come in. 'It's not me. I've someone to see you. Normally I don't encourage lady visitors to gentlemen's bedrooms but there's always an exception to prove the rule.'

From behind the middle of the huge frame of Guy's friendly but intimidating landlady a small, pale, slightly dirty face peered around. Before the landlady could beat a discreet retreat Maya was on top of Guy's bed with her arms wrapped around his neck. Guy started to cry. He tried to speak but couldn't.

It was Maya who spoke first. A rapid practical statement. There were no tears in her eyes but she was relieved beyond measure to be with the people she knew.

'I have been to the police. They brought me here. I have been walking all night. I want to go to sleep.'

'Of course. As soon as you want…but,' Guy couldn't resist asking, 'are you alright? Can you tell me what happened? Do you want to talk about it?'

'Yes.'

There was a long pause.

'Can I get you something? A cup of tea?' Guy winced as he asked the question. It seemed to be so hackneyed but he couldn't think what else to say.

Maya gave him a long sideways upwards glance. Then a broad smile broke across her anxious face. 'That would be lovely, yes.' She moved to sit demurely on the edge of the bed with her hands clasped tightly on her lap.

As if waiting in the corridor for her cue Mrs. Edwards appeared with two cooked breakfasts and a pot of tea for two. 'Hope you like full English dear. You look as though you could do with it. Bob's gone off down to Camelford for some hardware. He says he will be back in an hour.'

Maya muttered something about being very hungry although in fact she had already had a 'full English' or what she could bear to eat of it, kindly provided by the Police Station canteen. So she tucked in and thoroughly enjoyed the Italian tomatoes, delicate button mushrooms and soggy toast. She nibbled at the sausages and bacon but wasn't really keen. She wasn't vegetarian but just didn't fancy them much – at least not twice. The Police meal had been with baked beans. Guy nibbled at his breakfast too, as if embarrassed to make a pig of himself in front of her.

Maya said, 'Maybe you are right to value a simple cup of tea as a panacea to all the world's problems. It does represent the simple pleasures of life. The things worth celebrating are the things we share together without complication, without hidden motive, without greed. They are pure. Don't forget you picked up this habit from the East so I'm not likely to ridicule you for it. There is something similar in the Japanese tea ceremony but I don't know too much about that – that's not my cup of tea!'

She continued, 'It's a shame no-one smokes any more. There is something unbelievably seductive about a man lighting a cigarette for a lady. It expresses something intimate that mere words cannot convey. It was the black and white films I love. Of course I didn't realise then that they were all American but I liked the British war movies as well...'

'Maya', interrupted Guy sternly, 'tell me what happened.'

'Sorry. Just running off at the mouth. Glad to be able to.'

There was a catch in her throat. A tear welled in one eye but didn't come. 'As you know I had gone off on one of my little expeditions. I was curious, like the cat, but I guess I've used one of my lives now.'

'I had gone out on the coast path as usual but went up that valley by the stream. I was following a footpath in the direction of Port Quinn. There were some farm buildings and I thought I heard something or someone crying. I went to investigate and it was a tall barn with no access to where the crying was coming from. I didn't even try to speak or communicate with whatever was inside. The police said I should have called out and if there was no response to have walked away. In fact they say I should have walked away anyway. I'm sure they wouldn't have said that if it had been a baby or a child. Anyway it was a kitten. I didn't know that until I had climbed into the barn to find out. It was one of those barns that didn't have a door on the ground floor – at least I didn't see it. There must have been steps or a ladder but they weren't there. I had to climb up on a sort of winch. It was very dark inside but there was the kitten. The poor thing was hungry or frightened or cold or all three. I was just bending over it when I got an enormous thwack on the back of the skull.'

She turned to show Guy the site of impact. Even with Maya's thick black hair Guy could see the swelling and discolouration of the bruising at the base of her skull. Guy cradled her head around the ears with both hands as she turned to face him again. Maya answered his questions of concern with, 'the Police doctor said I was lucky. Because I was bending over he caught me at the base of the skull and the top of the shoulders with a glancing blow. It was still enough to knock me out and I also hit my head as I fell but he says if he had caught me full on the skull it would have broken or full on the neck it could have broken my spinal cord. He thinks it was a baseball bat or something similar.'

'Did you see the man?'

'No. I don't even know it was definitely a man and said so when the Police asked me. But I saw him later and I'm certain it was the same person. He must have thrown me or dropped me into the back of a pickup truck backed up to the barn as I remember getting a glimpse of bluey-black lines on his arm – probably a tattoo. Thinking about it though, there might have been two of them, because with a pickup truck backed up to the wall you could pretty much climb in there without the winch. One to drive, one to load. Maybe they used the winch to take me out. Who knows? The next thing I knew I was somewhere else. It could have been the farm across the yard or anywhere. It was dark. I was blindfolded. I was tied up to a thick wooden frame or post of some kind. It felt cold, wet and uncomfortable. There was the acrid smell of urine burning my nostrils. I realised it was my urine. I panicked and tried to cry out, banging my feet on the floor. I've always been a bit claustrophobic - you know, not being able to cope with being confined since my elder brother held me under some blankets as a child and I panicked because he was stronger than me and I couldn't get out or breathe properly. It was like that now. I couldn't breathe. I felt as if I couldn't get any air at all. 'Hyperventilating' I think the Doctor called it.'

'Nobody came. I struggled and struggled but all I succeeded in doing was making my ankles and wrists sore and bloody. I must have slipped into unconsciousness again, as the next thing I remember was the strong stench of somebody's breath in my face. It was rank with cigarette odour and food. Not garlic baguette but something pretty powerful. I tried to scream but I'm not sure if the sound came out properly or not. He disappeared pretty quickly and I could hear muffled conversation somewhere behind me. The first guy came back in and hit me across the face. He told me to be quiet. I couldn't help sobbing. I didn't want to. I didn't want to give them the satisfaction but I couldn't help it. I wet myself again. He laughed.'

'A long time seemed to pass and I was getting very faint. I realised I must be pretty dehydrated. There was a pain in the middle of my stomach that woke me. It was hunger as I have never experienced it before. It wasn't a gentle reminder to head for the fridge. It was an active physical pain like a finger being cut off. I called out but I don't think there was anyone there.'

'Another day must have passed. I lost track of time. There was no daylight but I could occasionally hear seagulls. When they stopped I knew it must be night.'

'A lot of thoughts passed through my mind. I had a lot of questions but no answers. I think I knew I wasn't going to die because I figured they wouldn't have taken the trouble to move me and yet I knew they wouldn't let me go and I was fairly certain they weren't going to give me anything to drink or eat. By this time it was just the drink that I craved. I couldn't summon any saliva to swallow and the air was hot and dusty. It was unbearable and I was beginning to panic again.'

'It was almost with relief that one of my captors came to see me. I couldn't see him (or her) as they stood behind me. There was a different smell with this one. Meat and fish. It was awful and yet pure. Like a cross between a butcher and a fisherman. The sort of smell that was masked with soap and disinfectant but you can never quite get it out of your skin, your fingernails, your hair and your clothes. I once took a job washing up at an Officer's Mess at an Army camp for some big function or visit they were having. It was like that. I smelled of Beef Wellington for days afterwards.'

'The person felt my hair. They pushed it back behind my ears. It was creepy but kind of tender. They went away and came back with a container of water. It had a sharp metallic edge and I cut my lip but I gulped the water down spilling it all around my throat and chest. I think it must have been an empty food can. I could taste something at the bottom of the water. It was like a combination of Baked Beans and meat. It hadn't been washed out. It made me feel sick and I was still thirsty.'

'I tried to speak. It was as if I hadn't spoken for weeks. The words were all jumbled but I wasn't trying to reason with them. I just wanted to know what was going to happen.'

'There was no answer. The person just went away.'

'I was really disappointed about this. I just wanted whatever was going to happen to be over. Even if it was going to be bad. I thought I would offer them something next time. I don't know what. Money. Anything. I had no pride. No dignity. Just life. Life I wanted to keep.'

'I tried to struggle free but I couldn't get my limbs to respond. I couldn't feel my legs anymore from the thighs down. My hands and my feet were completely cold as if my body were shutting down the parts it didn't need. I tried to shift my weight slightly in my torso. This was the nearest I could get to moving my muscles and getting any exercise so I made the most of it. I managed to generate a little bit of heat but it made me feel even more miserable. I couldn't help feeling it was so unfair. Why me? This is the sort of thing that doesn't happen in real life – at least not in Cornwall. It's supposed to be cream teas and what was that phrase you used?'

'Lashings of Ginger Beer,' responded Guy. 'I think my mother forced me to read too much Enid Blyton when I was growing up.'

'I began to wonder why they had tied me up, why they had moved me and what they intended to do. I had been trespassing, it's true, but I couldn't believe it was customary to tie up strangers on sight for that. Perhaps it was just opportunism. The person who came into the barn must be some sort of psychopath and hit me for no good reason or for being on his land. He regretted it and got scared, decided to hide the evidence, perhaps egged on by his friend. That was what worried me most: the fact that they were keeping me, like a fly in a web to be consumed later at their leisure. You know that spiders don't eat flies. They drink them.'

'I seemed to drift into a kind of torpor where nothing was possible anymore. There was no future. I was comfortably numb. But I knew this was dangerous. I tried to motivate myself to remember good things, good people, normal life. I thought about you – the kindness you had shown me, working with yourself and Bob. Don't laugh – I really needed to hold on to a sense of everyday normality. I seemed to alternate between extreme apathy, terror and anger. In the end it was anger that saved me. The anger that I still knew what should be normal and that these people had stolen it.'

'I think they must have moved me to some island because I could hear waves beating on at least three sides. Unfortunately I could also hear an animal in extreme pain. Don't ask me what a screaming puma sounds like but that was what it sounded like to me – some sort of big cat. There were a few muffled voices I heard and names. I think one was Prendick or something similar and the other one they called Doctor Bull. He was the one 'operating', as they called it, on the puma. He would do it in two hour stints – taking that poor beast to the brink of death and then saving or reviving it. Prendick was the only one that spoke to Bull – the others just grunted like hogs.'

'There may have been a leopard that died as well. On the next day, when they gave me some water, there was a bust up between them. At least I assumed it was the next day as time seemed to drag out to infinity and the amount of light never seemed to change. The Doctor got really angry with Prendick for killing a leopard. It had killed and half eaten his dog and Prendick had shot it. I don't know why. Revenge for killing his dog I suppose. Anyway Prendick stormed off saying he was going to hang out on Bodmin Moor and wouldn't be back to witness Bull's sick experiments. Bull told the two beast folk (as I now thought of them) to dump the two animal corpses out to sea using their boat and also 'deal' with me.'

'I was terrified they were going to take me out in their rickety boat. I've always had a horrible fear of choking and drowning. Another unfortunate childhood experience I expect. Anyway I must have fainted again at the thought of it or they had already given me something in the water to make me dopey. I had some sense of being moved. My face was sliding up and down on the floor of the pickup as I began to recover consciousness. We drew to a stop. The sound of the seagulls was even louder than the waves. I thought, Oh my God, they are going to throw me off the cliff instead. The back was opened. I closed my eyes and pretended to still be asleep. I knew I wouldn't be able run. My legs were still numb. Even with the adrenalin running I knew that I would only get one chance. I thought that chance would have to be by deception of some kind. I just hoped the opportunity would present itself … and soon. But that wasn't the way it happened. The smaller one pulled me out of the pickup and shouted something to the other to help. I half-opened one eye to get a look. The bigger one saw me and I saw him. He shouted something and moved to hit me again. I screamed and fell out of the truck and on to the floor. I was so angry I just shouted and shouted and shouted. All the hate, all the outrage, all the things they had put me through, all the worries and the pain all over my body just burst out of me like a torrent. What did they do? They just got back into the truck and drove off calmly as you like. I even think the big one was smiling.'

'I was still ranting and raving when some people turned up in, what looked like, space suits. For one moment I actually thought I was on a different planet. I don't remember anything they said. I was still 'spitting cobs' as my friend at College would say. They untied me and eventually put me into some sort of ambulance. They must have thought I was a complete lunatic. I'm surprised they untied me!'

'I was looked after at a tiny cottage hospital or GP's surgery – it wasn't a big place like Exeter. When I was feeling a little better and had been washed, clothed, re-hydrated, warmed up and generally sorted out they took me to a police station. They gave me another medical, took my statement, fed me sausages and brought me here.'

'Did they say anything?' asked Guy. 'I mean, did they know who the people were or what they were up to?'

'No. That's curious now I come to think of it. They just wrote everything down. Matter of fact. They didn't seem surprised.'

19. Saints with Attitude

Bob arrived with a huge bouquet of flowers, fruit and champagne for Maya. It was typically over the top. It was typically Bob. Maya was delighted and kept hugging Bob in embarrassed joy. The champagne went unopened. It was a little early even for Bob but there was a bit of a celebration and in no time at all it had stretched through into afternoon. Johnny and Marjorie had come over to pay their respects, as Guy had telephoned to say why no work would be done that day, and they invited Maya over to dinner. This was a very different Johnny to the one Maya had originally met. Maya declined the invitation though saying she was exhausted. She just wanted to go for a brief walk and test her new found freedom and then settle down for a quiet evening and early sleep.

She walked up out of the village, through the hedgerows, and onto the high farmland overlooking the bay. The tide was in and the fishing boats were nodding on the swell. By this time it was late afternoon on the threshold of a warm sultry evening with barely a breath of the fresh air she wanted.

Someone came hurrying up the path. She wondered if it was a jogger. Then perhaps she thought it was Guy or Bob not wanting her to be alone. 'Damn,' she thought, 'but I *do* want to be alone.' Then, as the person got closer, she realised with horror that it was Diggory Brae. He called out. Maya didn't respond. She realised she had nowhere to run but also, in a way, she didn't want to. He caught up to her and just stood there catching his breath.

He said, 'I've just heard what happened to you, I'm so sorry.'

Maya muttered something inaudible.

'I wanted to see if you were alright.'

Maya looked confused.

'You are alright, aren't you?'

'Yes.'

'Good. Good.'

There was a silence. They looked out to sea. Just standing side by side.

'Do you want to talk about it?' he asked.

'No.'

'Oh, okay.'

They continued standing to attention, side by side.

Diggory continued, 'I'm sorry about the other day, too. I guess I owe you an explanation. Not that there's much to tell.'

He waited in vain for a response then carried on. 'I didn't want you to find Ursell, my daughter who had come for a rare visit. She's on the run. Well, not "on the run" really, but she's upset an ex-boyfriend who is apparently…well, he's a bad'un, a bit dangerous. The only one who knows where she's now working is his new girlfriend Flo and she's heavily pregnant so I really hope he doesn't hurt her. There's just no thought, no planning. I don't blame her or Flo - it just makes me angry sometimes about young women no matter how lonely I get when no-one else is around.'

'Go on.'

'Well, when I met you I really liked you straight of and I thought maybe, well, I got the idea that we could be friends. I'm not really good at expressing this am I? Blokes don't do this sort of thing. Talk about emotions. Especially me. I never used to talk to my wife, not about anything important, and I really regret it now. She's gone. She died. It was…ghastly.'

'I heard about your wife.'

'You know about that?'

'Just that she died in a road accident and that you blamed yourself. I'm sorry.'

'No call for *you* to be sorry.'

'I just meant I'm sorry to bring it up.'

'Well, I was out working after we met, and I was thinking maybe I could drive you back into the village and we could go for a drink or something. There was nothing urgent I had to do in the evening that couldn't wait – even at this time of year. But then I realised how stupid I'd been.'

'What do you mean?'

'Well, no offence, but we don't get many people like you coming down here. We're a fairly insular lot. It occurred to me you might be connected with Ursell's Kevin. He's mixed up with some bad people. Some of them are Asian, or Chinese, or something. They drive around in a BMW with tinted windows and have those wraparound sunglasses where you can't see their eyes. I suddenly thought you'd been sent by Kevin and that was why you were being nice to me. You see, Ursell knows some things. Anyway I took her today to the police. She didn't want to go but I had to take her. That's where I found out about what happened to you. I said you were part of it. But you weren't, and I'm sorry; really really sorry.'

'Part of what?'

'The drugs and stuff, with that guy from Birmingham.'

'I don't know anything about it.'

'Yes, I know that now.'

They looked out to sea again, not at each other.

'Would you like to go for that drink now?'

'No, I think I just want to go back to the bed and breakfast and watch some mindless soaps on TV!'

So that's what she did. Diggory walked her back to the village. They spoke about the weather, tourism, farming, the weather,

Cornish Pasties and a bit more about the weather. When it came to saying goodbye Diggory bent down and gave her a brief kiss on the forehead. 'I'm sorry', he said again, turned and left. Maya watched as he walked swiftly down the street. He didn't turn around.

She sighed involuntarily. It wasn't to be. Not this time. Perhaps never.

'Why does two people meeting and enjoying each other's company have to be complicated by everyone else in their lives!' she said aloud and then muttered under her breath, 'I still fancy him rotten though.'

She opened the front door and walked into the lounge. She settled down in front of the telly with some chocolates Marjorie had sent over. She was completely relaxed but emotionally numb and drained. She even laughed as the blood spurted all over a nurse during a hospital series. It wasn't typical behaviour for her, it was just a temporary and welcome escape. Physical pain was now back safely behind the screen where it belonged. But later, when she retired to bed early, saying how tired she was the memory of her kidnap returned. Try as she might she couldn't sleep. She just kept tossing the bedclothes over her shoulder as she turned restlessly every few minutes. She couldn't forget, and she didn't see how she would ever forgive.

Maya woke Guy and Bob early to go onto site. She was determined to make up for lost time in the garden. She knew the delays that her disappearance and Bob's wrist had caused Guy. She knew how he must be rueing the cost. It was not a particularly auspicious start for the team and Maya wondered if she would ever get to work with them again. She knew Guy would be alright no matter what happened financially. He could always go back to his big job in the city or whatever it was. Bob seemed to get by with bits and pieces. His needs were probably modest – domestically. From what he had said he wasn't a great one for wanting a big house and all the paraphernalia of financial status. What was it he said? Something about 'settling for fast women and loose cars'.

Maya worked on savagely during the morning. Throwing her anger into effort. She also worked completely silently, wrapped up in her own thoughts, and the other two wisely kept chat to a minimum. Other than nods, grunts and pointing gestures Maya was the first to string a proper sentence together to start a conversation. 'What were you going to do here in the gravel in front of the bamboos?'

'I want Bob's driftwood sculpture to be the centrepiece of the design but I wanted something low to compliment it that you don't see from the top, that you only glimpse and have to walk down into the centre of the garden to see. I wanted to use a rowing boat but apparently they are in big demand. People put them on their ends and use them as little seats or arbours. I guess they are a bit clichéd now. It was Johnny who came up with the solution. He had some old bits and pieces from film sets but they were a bit flimsy and wouldn't have stood up to too much salt and sun. We selected a few bits and Bob has scattered those around the base – a couple of rusting ship instruments, some rope knots and so on. I mentioned the boat to Johnny and he said he that there was a farmer up near Port Gaverne that lets the long rowing boats, or gigs as they call them, park up before and after the sea races. There was one that was damaged by a tractor just before the last race. There was a bit of a fuss as it was one of the southern boats – not local. They said it was irreparable but the insurance company disagreed and wouldn't pay. They said it could be patched up. The rowers refused to go out in a damaged and repaired boat. They wanted a new gig. The thing had gone to the small claims court and the stupid thing was that they were looking to sell the boat to pay the legal fees. It seems such a shame. It would be a real waste to use it in a garden but there is not a lot of demand for these things other than from other teams and they jealously guard their own boats. It's very tribal. Needless to say I'm not going to turn it on its end and create a thirty foot arbour. We could, though, just about get it in to this gravel bed. It will make the bamboos look like riverside reeds. A bit like a silted up river bed in a quiet backwater of a coastal estuary.'

'I agree it seems like a waste. It should be kept as a workable boat if possible.'

'Will you come and have a look at it anyway?'

'Yes, I'd like that.'

After lunch the three of them drove up to the other side of Port Gaverne. They were told it was somewhere on the right. They overshot the farm, turned off the Gaverne road and went off up a side road to the right. Bob had taken the truck and they couldn't find a suitable place to turn around so they went on in the direction of the main A road past another farm and some rundown barns. Maya stared silently out of the window. At one point she seemed to catch her breath as if stifling a sob.

When they finally got back to Gaverne and found the right place Guy and Bob enthusiastically pulled back the cover to inspect the gig. They kept asking Maya to look at that, hold something, see this bit, but she was staring off in to the middle distance. Guy and Bob were like two little kids with a new toy – the only difference was that they weren't squabbling over who owns it. The farmer had left them to it but he now came out with the paperwork. He had all the papers from when the boat was commissioned, built, named, plus various safety certificates and regulations. It was like buying a car. Guy told him that they weren't interested in using it as a boat. That they just wanted the timber. The farmer's face fell. The only bright point for him was that it would stay in Cornwall. But at heart a farmer is a businessman and is no more sentimental about a gig than a tractor or a cow. Anyone who says they are not is a hobby farmer – someone who can afford to run rare breeds and make a few cheeses for the tourists. Even those lucky few are unlikely to turn down an honest profit. So the boat was sold. The gig owners couldn't afford to pay rent for storage to the farmer but they could offer him a commission for selling.

The farmer offered to deliver but in the end Bob borrowed a long trailer and somehow managed to attach it to back of his lorry. Maya had been standing by the road. She asked Guy if he minded if she went for a little walk. Guy told her that he wasn't going to let her out of his sight. 'Other than at night in bed' he added rather unnecessarily for the benefit of his audience.

There was an awkward silence.

Was Maya asking as an employee on company time? Or was Guy overstepping the mark? He did tend to be a little patronising and paternal. Well-intentioned but extremely irritating.

'Can I come with you?' he asked.

'How am I supposed to get this boat into the garden then?' piped up Bob before Maya could answer. 'I'll probably need some help getting it through the traffic and around corners as well.'

'You can put it in the main car park and we'll place it later when we've prepared the ground,' answered Guy.

There was another silence as Guy looked at Maya. She still seemed as if she was in a dream and not fully awake or, perhaps, it was a nightmare. 'Yes', she said finally.

Bob shrugged his shoulders and double checked the boat was secure. He revved the lorry up, a little theatrically, and pulled the boat out of the yard and down past the Headland Hotel and along the winding Port road.

Maya watched him go and then turned up the hill and started walking. Guy followed like an obedient dog a few paces behind. Neither spoke.

They walked on. What had taken a few seconds in the truck seemed to take forever on foot. As the ground rose they could get a better and better view of the sea behind them but they were mostly facing inland. Guy just looked down at his feet on the road, glancing at the grassy banks occasionally. Maya kept her head upright. She stared fixedly ahead, self-absorbed and grim.

In the distance they could see the pointed top of a gable from a house and attached barn beginning to emerge from over the rise. Behind them a car suddenly accelerated and skidded sideways to a halt blocking the road. Guy looked anxiously at Maya. Maya seemed unconcerned. She barely looked at the occupants of the car. They were two men. Guy looked them in the eye. They looked back unblinking. Maya walked on. Guy decided to follow.

They began to get closer to the farm. Guy kept looking over his shoulder although he tried not to. He pretended to look at flowers in the hedgerow as if the common lawn daisy was some new botanical discovery from a forgotten valley in the

Himalayas. Then he would throw a quick glance backwards. The men were just sitting there looking back at him.

Maya was getting increasingly ahead of Guy and was beginning to disappear around a slight bend. Guy hurried to try and catch up and almost ran into Maya who had suddenly stopped. She could see part of the yard now in front of the house. There was a man running across the front of the barn. He had a gun. There were cars in the yard. One of them was a police car. Looking back Guy saw that one of the two men in the black car that had stopped in the road behind them had got out of his car. He was carrying what looked like a sub-machine gun. Instinctively Guy called out in the direction of the police car. He wanted to run. In his mind he was running but his legs felt like concrete. The muscles in his leg ached with effort but he was completely stationary. It all seemed like a movie; as if he was watching events unfold without any means of influencing how they would turn out. He was a rabbit frozen in the onrushing headlights.

Maya looked at Guy. She saw the terror in his wide, astonished, eyes. She held his hand and spoke. 'I don't know what's going on but I'm glad. This is the farm where I was held. Don't ask me how I know, but I knew as soon as we passed it in the truck. It was the sounds and the smell of the place. Mostly the smell. You can smell it from here. The stench of rotting meat and shit.'

The man with the gun was now within a few yards. There was the sound of shouting and scuffling from the farmhouse. A large metal door was slammed against a wall and rang like a cracked bell. There was the sound of a van revving and it almost knocked Guy and Maya over as it screeched over the loose chippings and into the farmyard from in front of them. Somebody from the open window of the driver's side shouted, 'What the fuck are they doing here?'

Guy felt a pinching at his elbow. Maya shouted out in pain. The man from the car had grabbed them both by the arm and pulled them down to the ground. They ended up in one heap on the road with the man's gun (now strapped around his back) swinging forward and catching Guy in the chin with the barrel. When he had recovered his breath the man said, 'Sorry sir, it's not safe. I should have stopped you straightaway but I was waiting for identification and instructions.'

'You hurt my arm,' Maya said. Guy was speechless. He was checking whether his teeth were broken by running his tongue over them.

There was more shouting and banging from the farm. It sounded like a coach load of football hooligans had been thrown down a lift shaft, still chanting.

There was a crackling in the man's earpiece. He put his finger to it and frowned. The second man appeared from the car. 'It's a washout', he said.

'Yeah,' the other answered.

Soon afterwards there was more scuffling and the van that had nearly run them over before tried to get them again on its way out.

The man got up, leaving Guy and Maya on the ground, and melted back down the road. Both men they had seen before were now back in their car and drove off. Maya was already up and heading into the farmyard. Guy did his little dog act again and followed but a little more hurried this time and made sure to keep close. In fact he wanted to get in front of her.

Three men came out of the farmhouse next to the police car. Guy recognised one of them. It was the Customs investigator he had met at the Police station. 'What are you two doing here?' he asked.

'Maya recognised the farmhouse.'

Looking at Maya he asked with stinging sarcasm, 'Don't you think a little phone call to the police might have been the sensible thing to do?'

'I wasn't sure at first', she replied. 'I had to make sure. It was more a feeling than a certainty and I'm not a great one for women's intuition. Like you, I prefer facts.'

'Well, I had to tip off the guys in the road. Otherwise you'd have been flattened.'

Guy burst out, 'Sorry! I thought we were. Good job you hadn't told him we were the bad guys!' He added, 'They said it was a washout. What was?'

'Oh no. Far from it. In fact, as far as I'm concerned, it's the perfect result. It's true that whoever held you here, Miss Mai, has well and truly fled the nest. I think they had cleared up and were pulling out even before dumping you by the cliff path. That's why I'm so pleased. The... er... *special people* here might have wanted to feel someone's collar. Habeus corpus. Preferably the, what did you call them, oh yes, the bad guy's corpus or rather corpses. Me? I'm not interested in the couriers, and the bagmen and the lifters and shifters. I like evidence. Documents. Invoices, letters, photographs. That's what leads you to the real criminals – the people who make the money. I have a story to tell about them and none of the distractions of a wrongful arrest, a charge of excessive force or even a coroner's inquest. I'm not a great one for the Action Man stuff. It's the legal result I'm interested in. We have one arrest and a solid trail of evidence across Europe, Africa and Asia.'

'Who have you arrested?' asked Guy.

'The owner. "Bang to rights" I think they say on the cop shows. The farmer who lives here has a bit of a reputation. He's always looking out for tourists straying off the footpaths and over his land. He loves it. He gives them verbal abuse. Threatens them. And now we know why. We recovered Burmese pythons, star tortoises, turtles, cobras, rats, snakes, a monitor lizard and then 40 or 50 pieces.'

'40 or 50 species? That many!'

'No, pieces! Bits. Of animals. Beautiful leopard skins about three feet long, deer antler trophies, rhino horns roughly cut with half the nose still on, dried tiger penises, bear bladders. Stuff for traditional medicines from Thailand and Myanmar. We even found some old handwritten ledgers with all his accounts in. No names but plenty of dates and quantities to help us in our research. The old guy must have been running this business for decades.'

Looking at Maya Guy asked quietly, 'It's not the farmer we thought then?'

'No. Neither of them – not the bear baiter or the handsome young man you nearly tangled with in the Soupbine at Cold Comfort Farm. One of the local Bobbies knows Diggory quite well. He has just volunteered to act as a Special Constable and told us all about you, Miss Mai. He was a bit concerned about you. Said you were asking a lot of questions about the 'old religion'. Apparently his daughter knows some of those so called 'witches' up around Newquay as well as Boscastle and Port Isaac. He says they are mostly harmless – or at least as harmless as the Christians anyway. They have some strange parties, shall we say, but most of the time they are just ordinary nice people. That's the witches I mean, not the Christians. We were talking about it because there was one of those witches' shrines up near the cave that was being used for storing the animals. I asked Diggory and his daughter if any of those witches were likely to trade in exotic animal products for use in spells and ceremonies. I thought you might be the dealer we were looking for, and that was why you were asking about old myths and legends. He says that some of the hardcore witches, the dangerous ones, might buy unsavoury bits and pieces, but for most of them it was like a folk religion and so they would use traditional things readily available in the British countryside or 'grow your own' herbs and stuff. His daughter was even more emphatic that they were so much in awe of nature that it would be tantamount to blasphemy to treat wild animals like that. I wasn't so sure but they came across as pretty level headed and convincing. Ironic really that everyone around here thinks they are the ones that are a bit touched.'

'Mind you,' he continued, 'there was a linkup, in a way, with that bear baiting nonsense. The farmer near St. Endellion, that was in the papers about allegations of animal cruelty, was called Richard Trehayn.

I looked back in the files to find known associates from that time. There was nothing definitive on the bears but there were quite a few associates and drinking pals who were involved in cockerel and dog fights as well as some illegal hunting and livestock cruelty cases. I made a note of all these and there were two names that kept coming up again and again. One was a Birmingham businessman called Bull, or 'Bully', who was already into the summer drugs trade in Newquay and was looking for a piece of this as well.

The other was a local farmer called Kevin Penjerrick who had a suitably remote farm to hold some of the events. This Bull character had quite a rivalry with Trehayn, who he suspected of having an affair with his wife. Bull nearly cut her throat clean through and she still has a terrible scar on one side of her neck. People who know her say she's grown her hair long now and when she's nervous she tends to keep flicking it forwards with her hand over her shoulder or from her ear to try and cover it up. Meanwhile Bull sent his right hand man, Penjerrick, to sort out Trehayn. Penjerrick nailed Trehayn's favourite fighting dog through the throat to the cruck frame at the top of his own barn, and let him bleed to death. God knows how he got him up there. We'll have to ask him. We picked him up earlier in Bodmin with a train ticket for Birmingham. Didn't seem that keen on going though. He almost laughed in relief when we arrested him. Said he 'didn't want to go global', he 'wanted to stay local'.

Unfortunately we can't lock him up in Bodmin Jail with the rest of the dummies as it's a tourist attraction now. Even Dartmoor's too soft for him. He'll go to Exeter and then God knows where when he's sentenced. Birmingham's Winson Green I hope. One way or another, whether he's talkative or not, I'm sure he'll lead us back to Bull.'

'I think you've said enough Jonathan,' said the detective constable accompanying the Customs man. 'This is all still subjudice.'

'Okay. I just thought Miss Mai, at least, had a right to know that justice was going to be done. If not to the people who held her here then at least to their employees and the trade it represents. Incidentally it might interest you to know that the people who held you here couldn't speak English – one was Asian, possible Chinese or Korean, and the other was Eastern European, possibly from one of the ex-Soviet countries.'

'I'm not sure that's a comfort to Maya,' suggested Guy.

'It is comforting to know you are after them, but I don't think one of them was Chinese or Korean. Well not Mandarin speaking Chinese anyway, maybe Tibetan or Mongolian. I did swear at them in at least two languages and probably a third of my own invention. I would have thought he would have responded, if only to laugh at me. But for me, and I think for you too Jonathan, it's not so much about wanting to get my hands around the throat of the two idiots who held me, I just don't want anyone, or any creature, to be treated the way that I was. Is the tiger alright?'

'No. I'm afraid the vet had to put her down. They really would have done everything to save her if they could. Sorry.'

20. Lessons Learned

It was late when Guy and Maya had walked back in to Port Isaac and the crimson and orange sunset was stunningly clear across an hundred and eighty degree horizon as they passed the gig in the car park. Luckily it was parked after 6pm so there was no charge until the morning. It took up the equivalent of eight car spaces so it would have come to a tidy sum.

Maya stopped and looked out to the triangular rock rising straight out of the sea at Trebarwith Strand and beyond towards the castle on the headland at Tintagel, now brightly lit in an orange-bronze glow. The sound of the gulls wheeling noisily on the cliffs below added rather than detracted to the sense of unbelievable calm. It was over. She could relax. It was like sinking into a hot bath of warm coastal air. As it slipped silkily across her neck she could feel the muscles in her shoulders soften and unwind.

Guy stepped up behind her and placed one hand on hers. His other hand lightly rested on her right shoulder.

Maya turned to face him. 'You still love your wife Julie, don't you?'

'Yes, of course I do. You don't spend that long loving someone and then just stop. The only difference is that I hate her now as well.'

'Good.'

'Which? Hating her or loving her?'

'Loving her. That has to be good doesn't it?'

There was a long moment's hesitation and then he said, 'Come on – we've got a garden to finish and we'll have to be up early to move the boat before the car park attendant gets here.'

They walked in silence back to the B&B. It was a cup of hot chocolate and early to bed. Two beds. Two rooms.

Bob came in noisily, quite late. He was well oiled with St. Austell's finest brew. Guy was woken momentarily. Maya slept through, very deeply, and awoke completely refreshed. In fact Bob was the first up and seemed none the worse for his booze cruise around the harbour. They got the gig out before the tourists started to arrive but a few fishermen and local traders were setting up for the day's work. Bob backed the lorry up to the garden by almost jack-knifing the trailer in the narrow road to give it a reasonable angle of approach. Guy and Maya, the latter on tip toe, lifted the rim of the gig over the hedge above the dwarf wall. The springiness in the privet branches lifted the hull clear of any obstacles. Guy then rushed into the garden to guide the prow into place. There was an awkward moment when it reached the balance point and like a see-saw began to rise rapidly off the trailer at one end and fall into the garden at the other end. Guy and Maya had rigged up some bags of compost and a few straw bales borrowed by Johnny from a local stable. Fortunately the gig fell onto this – although it did slide sideways and end up at a rather ungainly and rakish angle slewed on its left side.

Guy looked anxiously along the hull where it had come to ground. He was concerned in case the gravel had scored the wood and so, crouching in a semi-squatting position, he proceeded rapidly to bounce along the length of the gig with his elbows flapping up and down like chicken wings to retain balance.

Maya couldn't help bursting out laughing and that set Johnny and Marjorie off who had rather nervously been watching from the open patio door. Maya got the giggles really badly. She was in tears and her chest hurt. She managed to gasp, 'Is it a bird…or a plane?'

Bob, who had poked his head around the corner of the hedge to see what the commotion was, helpfully suggested, 'I think it's a pregnant duck with a haemorrhoid problem'.

Everyone burst out laughing again. Even Guy permitted himself a small twist of a smirk as he straightened up, followed by a demure titter, followed by a short, but gutsy, guffaw.

When they were all safely returned to a dignified silence Johnny sidled up behind Guy and confided, 'I know you said you'd probably have to cut the end off to get the boat in the right place…'

'Yeesss,' said Guy, warily.

There was a pause.

'I don't want you to cut it.'

'Why?'

'Because it's a boat.'

'You don't seriously expect it to go out to sea again do you? It's damaged.'

'Yes, but it's repairable and it looks like a boat. If we cut the end off it's not going to be a boat. It's going to be a pile of bent wood.'

Guy thought about this for a while. He considered putting the gig diagonally across the garden but it would be on a slope and he didn't think it would look right. A boat has to be on the level – as if it were resting on the water. He had made a gravel stream bed and wanted to maintain the feeling of a boat resting on the shore or, where the bamboos were, of a punt cutting through the reed beds. The problem with keeping the boat on the level was that the end would go straight across the central pond. Guy walked over to the pond and squatted down. Then he took two steps back and lay flat on his stomach. Maya wondered if he was going to treat the audience to another funny little dance when he sprang up and turned to Johnny.

'It could work. The pond is recessed into ground level. As long as we keep the boat on some blocks to stop it rolling it should just come level with the pond. From above it will look as though it is sitting in the water but without actually having to sit in it. We will need to cut a hole in the hedge and have one end of the boat disappearing into the neighbour's garden like a gondola going under a bridge. I think it will look great from both sides of the hedge and I know it will solve a problem for your neighbour. It will be like sharing a drainpipe. It will be alright as long as he doesn't paint his end pink. When I first came here I had to placate your neighbour who turned out to be a really nice bloke. He was quite pleased that you were having your garden done up. He did say, though, that it would be nice to have some hold over Johnny's behaviour and now I think he has it. Any misdemeanours and he would be able to have the other end of the boat removed. In fact I'm tempted to dig a little ditch all the way back to the hedge on the top side of the boat where you will see it from the house and fill it with water like a moat.'

'Won't it look silly or twee if it's a small channel.'

'No. I don't think so. We'll make the edges natural. It will be like a little stream emptying onto the sea with the boat resting by the side of the stream on the shore as if ready to launch. I'm not going to dig too deep for the trench – just lift the gravel and put waterproof membrane offcuts under it and then mask it by putting some of the gravel back down. Fortunately I'd already chosen fairly well-rounded stone gravel that could pass for riverbed if you look at it from any distance… with a bit of a squint.'

So they set to work putting in the extra water feature. It was all additional work at no additional profit but Guy felt he had to finish it off and he had the materials to do it. With Bob being a little more active it even went quite quickly. Marjorie also came out to help with topping up some of the gravel. Towards the end Guy could even afford the luxury of acting as supervisor, keeping the pegs and lines straight whilst the others laid the material and planted round it.

When they were standing back admiring their work Guy asked Marjorie the question he had been dying to put to her, 'how did you know the child's hand was something to do with the vicar?'

'Being on the Flower Show sub-committee is a bit like being on the Church Council, both of which I'm a member. You get to know your exhibitors like you know your parishioners. I knew he was up to something with those boys. I'd seen him sneaking off with them. But unlike the rest of the village I knew he was unlikely to be after sex.' Marjorie looked at the ground and, with her eyes still turned slightly downward she continued, hesitatingly, 'I knew this because ...I had a bit of a flirt with him when he first arrived.' Then she looked Guy fully in the eyes, 'Johnny was being particularly irritating that year and I was lonely. Tom was so full of ideas and energy and enthusiasm when he first arrived. He was a real breath of fresh air in this community. Anyway you probably don't need to know it but, believe me, *that* man was definitely a woman's man. Unfortunately it emerged he was much more of a *women's man* than a *woman's man*.'

'What do you mean?'

'I eventually agreed to go away with him for a romantic weekend only to find he had booked me into a room with three other female friends. So, reluctantly, I ended it before it had really begun. Besides, I regretted the possibility that I could seriously hurt Johnny. He's a funny little man but he keeps me amused. This garden, in a way, was one of the ways in which I have been attempting to say sorry.'

'But how did you know about the child?'

'Oh easy, I recognised the mole on his knuckle. It was our best singer, and his favourite allotment helper. A really sensible boy. He could win a music scholarship if he doesn't get distracted. I knew he wouldn't be stupid enough to have thought of doing something like that on his own. It had to be Tom and maybe the other boy that had put him up to it in some mad attempt to sabotage the other allotments.'

'May seem obvious to you. It didn't to me. So it was the mole in the hole that undermined him.'

'That's a particularly weak set of puns even for you Guy. I guess when I hit Tom I was angry about him putting the child in danger but there was a bit of personal revenge, as well, for making me feel foolish. I don't feel good about that. I'm surprised he hasn't asked for the police to charge me with assault.'

'I think he'll probably carry enough guilt for both of you so I wouldn't worry about that too much. Are you sure Johnny is worth the spoiling?'

But, before Marjorie could comment, Bob distracted both of them by emulating Guy's careful examination of the gravel levels. He put his head on one side, closing one eye and giving it a bit of a leer while flapping his elbows. Johnny and Maya, who were now standing side by side at the other end, almost arm in arm, shared a mutual grin.

Guy and Marjorie also exchanged glances. Marjorie understood what was now on Guy's mind. He was thinking back to when Johnny had been so rude about Maya's involvement in the project. Marjorie felt honour bound to remind Johnny of his previous attitude to Maya. Marjorie didn't often take the moral high ground with Johnny. She knew it was a waste of time. But when she wanted to take the opportunity to perform the coup de grace she did it with relish and venom.

'Nice to see you two getting along so well. Do you remember what you first said about Maya coming to do the garden?'

Even Johnny, not normally noted for his sensitivity, glowed bright red through from his neck to his cheeks as if a giant pair of red phosphorus match heads had been ignited in his mouth.

Marjorie continued, like a huge oil tanker unable to change direction in anything less than two miles. She was now heading towards Johnny, only yards away and there was no stopping her beaching on his shore. 'Slanty-eyed what was it? Oh yes, slanty-eyed bint you called her.'

There was a horrible silence. Even the blackbirds didn't dare make a sound. Then Johnny began to clear his throat. Maya just looked weary, bored and a little embarrassed by it, as if she would rather be somewhere else.

'That was before I met her. You have to understand that people of my generation have a different world view. We were brought up in a time when the Germans and the Japanese weren't known for making cars efficiently, they were known for torturing and killing efficiently.'

Marjorie spluttered, 'Your experience of the Japanese, and by the way Maya isn't Japanese in case you hadn't noticed, was from a stand-in part in Tenko.'

'No. That's not true. I've played a number of parts about the war in the Pacific and, unlike many so called professionals that I worked with, I do my research. I have read extensively, as you well know, and did so long before I met you. Anyway the point is I admit to being prejudiced. I am not proud of it but there is a reason. I don't believe any amount of political correctness can make wrong appear right, or make a nation or a people suddenly okay.'

Guy joined in, 'But the whole point is we are not governments or races. We are individuals and should be judged according to our own unique set of views, attitudes and behaviours. No-one has the right to say what we are just by how we look. The more homogenised we become in our jeans and t-shirt uniforms the more difficult and the more circumspect people should be.'

'Yes. You're right. I didn't know Maya. I know a little of her now. And the more I know the more I like and respect her. I'm sorry,' he turned to face her, 'I'm really, really sorry.'

Maya said, 'I can't forget what you said. It's a horrible thing to say and to think. But I can forgive. Isn't that what reconciliation and peace after war is all about?'

'Can you forgive what those people, who kidnapped you, did to you?' asked Johnny.

'No. In all honesty I can't. They just kidnapped me because I was an inconvenience to them. I was in the wrong place at the wrong time and they must have thought I knew or had seen something. I don't hate them though. Hate just poisons and rots the person who feels it. But I can't understand why they did what they did. I don't want to understand it. There's no excuse. I tried to think of it as a good life experience. A resetting of priorities, a way of strengthening my appreciation of the good things – like the friendship I've known here. But, even so, I can't say I'm a better person for the experience. I'm simply not. It destroyed any sense of security I had, of any belief in the basic goodness of people. I thought I could forgive. I even thought that, like Endellienta, I could meet someone evil and somehow bring them back to life. I guess I'm not as good as I thought I was.'

'So remind me again what happened to that Endellienta person?'

'I found a story about her by Nicholas Roscarrock and I suppose I became a bit obsessed with finding out more about the places that had given rise to the story. She lived a very austere life, with a single cow, and was said to live on milk and water from two nearby wells. Her sister had come to live at nearby St. Illich, which I didn't know where it was but wondered if it had something to do with Isaac; knowing how names can change slightly over the centuries. Anyway the two would meet along a path between Port Isaac and what is now known as St. Endellion where it was said the grass grew greener than anywhere else. Unfortunately Endellienta's cow was killed by the Lord of Trenteny when it had strayed onto his land. Trenteny was punished and killed but Endellienta didn't want anyone murdered because of her and is said to have brought him back to life.'

'So if you'd had the chance, you would have brought your captors, or whoever was behind them, back to life?'

'I don't know. I'm not, in any sense, a saint; either by being that good or being handy with miracles.'

'Good,' said Johnny, as if relieved that there was no-one in the room better than him. 'You might be interested in this article from the local rag then.'

Johnny handed a creased, roughly torn, piece of newspaper to Maya. Guy and Bob looked over her shoulders as she read the headline out, 'Two bodies recovered from stricken vessel.'

It was an account of a small boat, rather than what any seafarer would call a 'vessel'. It had apparently capsized in stormy

231

weather off the coast of North Devon. The bodies hadn't been identified but were two males. One was a short Asian man with close cropped hair, the other was tall, long haired, had a damaged ear where an earring may have been ripped off and had a twisted rope design tattooed on the right forearm. But the boat was unregistered and unidentifiable. The paper speculated that, judging by the state of their clothes and lack of equipment, they were neither fishermen nor tourists, and appealed for anyone who knew of any missing persons to come forward. So far, no-one had.

'Do you think that might be them?'

Johnny answered a question with another question. 'Would you like it to be them?'

'For revenge? No, not really. I'm curious, that's all.'

Marjorie said, 'I remember being on jury service once. We brought back a verdict but we never got to hear what the sentence was. I felt cheated that we never got the satisfaction of knowing for sure that they were punished.'

'Oh yes,' said Johnny, 'I remember you telling me about that. A Brummy child molester. They should have sent him down for his accent alone.'

The rest just looked at him, slightly opened mouthed, but for Johnny there was only so much political correctness you can put up with in one day.

'Okay Tonto,' said Bob turning to Guy, 'time for us to be heading off into the setting sun.'

Guy had to point out that there was nothing but thousands of miles of sea if they headed off into the setting sun. Also, home was in the opposite direction. And he wasn't called Tonto. Otherwise it was an excellent suggestion and the three of them were happy to act upon it.

Ade Annabel describes himself as "a carbon based lifeform from somewhere near Goonhilly".

He is also a married man with two sons, lives in the UK and has worked in the Arts, Horticulture and Information Technology. He has written articles for a number of newspapers and magazines and in his spare time enjoys playing a wide range of musical instruments fairly badly.